IN ME

NEW YORK TIMES BEST SELLING AUTHOR

SAMANTHA CHASE

"If you can't get enough of stories that get inside your heart and soul and stay there long after you've read the last page, then Samantha Chase is for you!"

-*NY Times & USA Today Bestselling Author* **Melanie Shawn**

"A fun, flirty, sweet romance filled with romance and character growth and a perfect happily ever after."

-*NY Times & USA Today Bestselling Author* **Carly Phillips**

"Samantha Chase writes my kind of happily ever after!"

-*NY Times & USA Today Bestselling Author* **Erin Nicholas**

"The openness between the lovers is refreshing, and their interactions are a balanced blend of sweet and spice. The planets may not have aligned, but the elements of this winning romance are definitely in sync."

- ***Publishers Weekly, STARRED review***

"A true romantic delight, *A Sky Full of Stars* is one of the top gems of romance this year."

- ***Night Owl Reviews, TOP PICK***

"Great writing, a winsome ensemble, and the perfect blend of heart and sass."

PROLOGUE

WILLIAM MONTGOMERY WAS FEELING PRETTY good about himself.

And with good reason.

As the orchestra played, he watched his youngest son Lucas dancing with his new bride, Emma. They made a beautiful couple and as far as William was concerned, his role as matchmaker was a complete success.

Looking around the room, he saw that everyone was laughing, smiling, and having a good time. It filled his heart with joy. This time last year, Lucas was a brooding loner who had cut himself off from just about every aspect of life. But thanks to William's interference, and the help of Mother Nature, Lucas had found himself and fallen in love with the beautiful Emma Taylor, now Emma Montgomery. William had no doubt that there'd be a grandchild in the near future.

A server came over to refill his champagne, and William smiled at him. Why hadn't he thought to do this before? He had three sons who seemed content to stay single. Well, now he had only two to worry about, but still...

Mac and Jason were both over by the bar talking with some business colleagues, and he frowned. Why were they talking business when there were eligible women in the room? Hell, why were they talking business at all while at a wedding? Where had he gone wrong?

William sighed wearily. His sons seemed clueless where women were concerned, at least as far as he could tell. Not that he thought either of them was living the life of a monk, but it would be nice if one of them had a girlfriend.

Or at least a date for their brother's wedding.

"Stop frowning, William, it's our son's wedding." His beautiful wife of thirty-five years came and sat down beside him, placing a gentle kiss on his cheek. "There's nothing to frown about today."

"Says you," he mumbled.

"What could you possibly have to be unhappy about? Emma and Lucas are deliriously happy and in love. The wedding is lovely and everyone is having a good time." Stepping in close, she hooked her arm with his and smiled. "It's a perfect day. Look at how happy they look!" She pointed to the bride and groom. "Have you ever seen Lucas look like that?"

Wordlessly, William shook his head.

"I never thought this day would come," she went on. "I thought for sure that Lucas was going to just hole up in that cabin in the mountains and cut himself off from everything and everyone."

"He almost did."

"Well... I didn't fully agree with you at the time, but now I know that you were right. All he needed was a little nudge."

Kissing the top of his wife's head, William tried to smile, but... he couldn't.

"Look at them." He motioned to their sons by the bar.

"Mac and Jason? What about them?" she asked.

"When are they going to find women and fall in love and get married?"

"Oh, William, for crying out loud. We're not even done with this wedding and you're already trying to plan the next one?" she laughed. "Can't we breathe a little first?"

"I just want to see them happy."

"Who says they're not?"

"Do you remember Lucas a year ago?" he asked, taking his eyes from his sons to focus on his wife.

"You cannot compare Jason and Mac to what Lucas was going through; the situations are completely different."

"On some levels, yes. But basically, they are too wrapped up in business to have relationships. I don't want them to work their lives away. They deserve to have the kind of love that Lucas and Emma have, and that you and I have."

She smiled and cupped a hand to her husband's cheek before leaning in and kissing him softly on his lips.

"What was that for?"

"For being wonderful."

He smiled. "I know that for a while Lucas wasn't thrilled with me for interfering in his life, but maybe this time..."

"Don't you dare!" she scolded. "You were lucky where Lucas and Emma were concerned. They already had feelings for one another. You just had to nudge them along. Neither Jace nor Mac are in that position."

"Not yet," William said.

"I think it's wonderful that you helped Lucas and Emma. I look at the two of them and it just fills my heart with joy."

"But?"

She smiled serenely. "But... I think all things happen for a reason. And some things shouldn't be interfered with."

"Nonsense. I'm not going to do anything."

"You do remember that your little matchmaking scheme almost failed, right?"

"Almost," he said with a grin. "I didn't expect Lucas to be so openly hostile."

"You cost Emma her job with Montgomery's, William."

"Believe me, I know that, but I can't be sorry for it. You have to admit that it all worked out for the best! Emma has her bakery, Lucas finally had the surgery on his knee, and by this time next year, you and I could be grandparents!"

Her smile grew. "I do like the thought of that." Looking over her shoulder, Monica sighed softly as she watched Lucas and Emma dance.

"And that's just the beginning," he murmured close to her ear before placing a soft kiss on her cheek. "Imagine how many more grandchildren we could have if our other sons spent a little less time in the boardroom and a little more time in the..."

Monica put her hand over his mouth. "Oh, hush." Then she kissed him. "You're going to do what you're going to do and nothing I'm going to say will stop you, right?"

"Well..." he began sheepishly.

"Just... behave," she told him. "And maybe take the rest of the weekend off from this new hobby of yours before getting into any trouble. At the very least, enjoy our son's wedding." And with a serene smile, Monica stood and went to talk with some of their guests.

Taking a sip of his champagne, William looked over at Jason and Mac again. They were good men—good looking, hardworking, and brilliant businessmen. They'd make an excellent catch for any young woman.

"If I could just get them to get out of work mode once in a while, maybe they'd find someone."

The thought was almost laughable.

It had taken the situation with Lucas and Emma for William to realize two things.

First, just how deeply seated his sons were in their jobs.

And while it was commendable and something he had raised them to be, he was beginning to think that maybe he'd done too good of a job instilling a solid work ethic in them. Neither one seemed to know how to take a step back from the office and just relax!

And second, just how deeply seated they were in their bachelorhood.

And that was definitely no longer a good thing.

He wanted to see them all happily married with families of their own. He knew he wasn't getting any younger and if he didn't do something soon, he'd be too old to enjoy his grandchildren. And if Mac and Jason weren't willing to actively find themselves brides, then it was up to him to lend a helping hand.

Whether they wanted it or not.

Come Monday morning, he was going to actively begin searching for his next daughter-in-law.

"Congratulations, William! Lucas and Emma are both positively beaming!" his good friend Arthur said as he approached. "Mind if I join you?"

He motioned to the chair beside him. "The more the merrier!" They tapped glasses. "To the happy couple!"

Arthur agreed. "I've never seen Lucas look happier."

William Montgomery was feeling good about himself

right now. He had a purpose and a plan was beginning to form.

All he needed was for lightning to strike twice.

ONE

"SHE HAS TO BE MARRIED."

"Excuse me?"

"Whoever it is we choose, she has to be married." Jason Montgomery was adamant on this point. There was no way he was going to get caught with someone else looking to snag the wealthy boss.

"This is about Lucas, isn't it?" The head of human resources eyed him with a mix of suspicion and humor. In her late fifties, Ann Kincade had been with Montgomerys for almost twenty years and had watched Jason and his brothers grow up. "Honestly, Jason, you are making a big deal out of nothing."

"Am I?" he asked incredulously. "Ever since Lucas and Emma got together, I have gone through four assistants. Why? Because now they all think they can hook up with the boss."

"That's a slight exaggeration, Jason," she admonished. "They haven't all been like that."

"Is it? Really?" He stood and began to pace his office. "First there was Rose—"

"Rose got promoted to being your father's assistant when Emma left. That had nothing to do with you. She's happily married and never once even implied anything inappropriate."

Jason sighed with frustration. "That wasn't what I was going to say. When Rose moved over to the main suite, you replaced her with Janice."

"She was a very nice woman. Great organizational skills."

"She was a damn stalker who I found watching me through the bushes at home with binoculars!" He let out a small growl of frustration. "I had to install security cameras after that incident!"

"Okay, I'll give you that one. But then there was Lynda—"

"Cougar on the prowl. She didn't want to work; she wanted to find a rich, *younger* husband to take care of her."

"And her typing skills sucked."

One of Jason's eyebrows arched at that comment, but he said nothing.

"Then there was Claire." He stopped and stood in front of Ann his arms crossed over his chest. "Do I even need to remind you of that little debacle?"

Ann looked down at her pile of files in her lap. "I still think it wasn't what it looked like."

"The woman was sprawled out on my desk in her underwear. How could that be misinterpreted?" he shouted.

"There could have been a medical emergency and you just happened to walk in while she was... you know... posing like that."

A growl of frustration escaped before he could stop it, and

he raked a hand through his hair. "Now I have this trip coming up that I need to take an assistant on and I don't have an assistant! I'm walking around on eggshells here because I feel like everywhere I turn, there is someone looking to marry me!"

This time, she did snicker, and when he glared at her, she simply cleared her throat and did her best to look contrite.

"We'll have to put an ad out and look for male assistants," Ann suggested.

"There's no time for that, and what if he's gay?"

Ann let out a hearty laugh before she could help it. "Oh, Jason, do you hear yourself? Now you think that men are going to be after you, too?"

He sat back down behind his desk and put his face in his hands. "I'm going crazy here, Ann. I have a lot to do to prep for this trip. There's so much riding on it and I can't spare the time to fend off women who are hoping to be the next Mrs. Montgomery."

"Is it absolutely necessary for you to have someone go with you?" she asked seriously. "Can you possibly just call in with updates and maybe Rose can take care of things? I know it's not ideal, but...

"It's a long trip, with meetings set up with dozens of potential clients. As it is, I've had to do all the scheduling myself because I haven't had anyone stick around long enough to actually work." Letting out a long breath, he leaned back in his chair. "I need someone to be with me taking notes, organizing contracts, and getting them back here to the office. I can't do it all myself. As it is, this went from a ten-day trip to about three weeks. What am I supposed to do?"

"That's a long time to ask anyone to travel with you,

especially if they're married. No one is going to want to be away from their spouse for three weeks."

Jason frowned. "Damn, I hadn't thought of that."

Ann started sorting through the employment profiles she held in her lap. "As of right now, there are no male candidates. You could always take one of the junior execs with you to—"

Jason shook his head. "No, the ones I talked with can't be spared for that length of time."

"What about a temp?"

Again, he shook his head. "I need someone with a working knowledge of the company. I won't have time for training. I need someone who can step right in and get to work. I've got less than two weeks before I leave, and I'll need every minute of it to get organized."

Placing the files down on Jason's desk, Ann stood and frowned. "What you're asking is impossible."

"I'm relying on you to make it possible," he countered.

She gave him a patient smile. "I can appreciate what you're trying to do, but I'm not a miracle worker. I can't pull the perfect candidate from thin air." She paused and shook her head. "I have been combing through all the departments and no one meets your criteria."

"Someone does," he countered. "There has to be. I'm not asking for all that much."

"You're asking for too much." Another pause. "Jason, be reasonable."

"I would love to be reasonable, Ann, believe me. Right now, there is nothing about this situation that makes things easy for me, either. I cannot afford to take someone with me who 'accidentally' shows up in my bed or, worse, makes a spectacle of themselves at a corporate event. I don't want to lead anyone on or give them the impression that they are with me to play corporate wife!"

She stared at him until Jason felt like he was going to squirm.

"I'll see what I do, Jace, but I can't make promises."

He nodded, and then she was gone.

With a ragged sigh, he spun his chair and stared out at the city skyline. "Why does this have to be so damn difficult?"

He fully blamed his brother.

If Lucas hadn't gone and married Emma, none of this would be happening. Hell, before the two of them hooked up, keeping assistants hadn't been an issue. But now? He let out a low snort. The examples he'd given Ann had been the worst of the worst. In between, there had been countless temps who he just didn't click with.

There was a part of him that realized he was being overly critical and he really didn't envy Ann's position in all of it, but... he was determined to make a name for himself at Montgomery's.

And not just the name he inherited by being born into the family.

His father was brilliant, and so were Mac and Lucas. But as the middle child, Jason had always felt like people tended to overlook him like he wasn't there. Maybe he wasn't as brilliant as Mac or as successful as Lucas, but he was his own man, dammit. And if he could make this project of a success and bring in the number of clients he was leaning toward, no one would be able to overlook him again.

It had to succeed. It just had to.

He just needed the right person at his side to make it happen.

~

Maggie Barrett did her best to live her life under the radar.

Getting called into the boss's office did not fit with that motto.

Not even a little bit.

She had barely stepped into the executive suite when William Montgomery's assistant, Rose, told her that Mr. Montgomery was expecting her. With a heavy sigh, and a straightened spine, she walked through the doors.

"Maggie!" William Montgomery boomed. "How have you been?"

Taking the seat he showed, Maggie sat down and swallowed the nervous lump in her throat before responding. "Fine, sir. How are you?"

"Great, can't complain," he said with a sincere smile, and then he reached for a folder that was on his desk. His expression turned slightly more serious as he read the contents. Quietly, he closed the folder and studied her. "Ann tells me you were offered a promotion."

Maggie nodded. "Yes, sir, I was."

"And that you turned it down."

Again, she nodded.

"Care to tell me why?"

"I'm perfectly happy with the position I have." She did her best to sound confident, but there was a slight tremble in her voice that she couldn't hide.

"You are overqualified for the position you have, Maggie, you and I both know that. Now, why don't you tell me why you really turned down the job as Jason's assistant?" His tone was firm but gentle.

Her shoulders sagged slightly. "You know why I took this job, Mr. Montgomery. I'm not looking to be anyone's assistant ever again." There. That time she definitely sounded confident. "I'm very happy working in customer service."

"Answering phones all day is maddening," he replied with a frown. "The move up to an assistant would mean that other people would field the calls, and you could do the kind of work that you are more than capable of doing."

It probably wouldn't look good for her to cry in front of her boss. Not that he hadn't seen her do that before, but it wasn't something she wanted to repeat. "I appreciate your concern, Mr. Montgomery, I really do. I'm just not willing to be put into that type of situation ever again. I can't." Her voice trembled again on the last word and Maggie silently cursed herself for showing weakness.

"Maggie," he began hesitantly, softly, "I am not the type of person who throws his weight around. I think you know that about me."

She nodded.

"We have a rather... delicate situation that you are the only one qualified for. I'm not asking you if you want the position, I'm telling you that I want you to take the position."

Maggie's head snapped up as she stared at him with eyes wide. "But you know why—"

William held up a hand to stop her. "Believe me, I remember quite well why you feel the way you do, and I think that by now you should know that I am one of the good guys. Have I ever done anything to make you doubt me?"

Silently, Maggie shook her head.

"Have I asked anything of you in all the time you've worked for me?"

Again, she shook her head as she stared down at the floor.

"I wouldn't ask this of you if it wasn't important. You are the only person I can trust for this assignment."

Raising her head, her brown eyes filled with tears, she asked, "Why? Why me?"

William sighed. "Well... ever since Lucas and Emma fell in love, Jason has had sort of a target on his back. We can't seem to keep an assistant for him. He's been stalked, hit on, propositioned... you name it, these women have done it. Most men would be flattered, but Jason takes his work very seriously and he needs someone who'll do the same."

"I still don't understand how this involves me."

"When I took you in with Montgomery's, Maggie, you asked me to do what I could to protect you, right?"

Again, she nodded.

"One thing that I did was lie for you. As far as anyone in the company knows, you are a married woman. You and I are the only ones here who know differently."

Maggie considered his words. "So, you think since everyone believes me to be married that I'm a safe bet for Jason's assistant?"

"That's exactly what I'm thinking. Jason isn't looking to seduce anyone and he certainly isn't looking to be seduced. He's feeling more than a little cagey and can't seem to relax in his own office. I hate it for him, believe me. And I would think that you, more than anyone, can understand his position."

She blushed. Maggie tried never to think about how she had come to work for William Montgomery, and in the three years she'd been here, this was the first time they'd referred to it. "I can respect the situation, sir; I just don't feel comfortable..."

"Maggie?" he interrupted gently. "It's time. You've hidden yourself down in customer service long enough. I hired you without knowing a damn thing about you. The woman I met needed help, and I gave it. I'm asking you to return the favor."

How could she say no to that? The man had given her a safe haven, a job where she didn't feel hunted, or that she was there for any other reason than her work. "How can I be sure I won't find myself in the same situation I was in when you met me?"

William's expression softened as he looked at her. "Maggie, I give you my word that you will never, *ever* find yourself in such a position. Not with Jason and not with anyone here at Montgomery's." He gave her a reassuring smile. "But especially not with Jason," he added. "I raised him to respect women and his reputation speaks for itself."

"Can I have a few days to think about it?"

His smile was sympathetic. "Unfortunately, time is of the essence right now. This project my son is working on requires immediate assistance." He paused. "Can I count on you, Maggie?"

She stood and looked down at her boss. A simple nod of her head was the only response she gave.

William rose to his feet and faced her. "If at any time, for any reason, you feel like something isn't right, I want you to promise me you'll call. I'll believe whatever it is you tell me and I'll get you out of there, no questions asked, okay?"

Again, all she could do was nod.

"I'll let Ann know to get the paperwork started. I'll also let Rose know that you'll be working with her the rest of the week to get acquainted with things up here and arrange for you to meet with Jason."

"Um... alone? I mean... will Rose be with us? Or... or..."

A wild look of panic crossed Maggie's face and William made a quick decision. "We'll meet with him together, you and me, okay?"

Maggie took a steadying breath and agreed.

Then silently prayed that she hadn't just made the second biggest mistake of her life.

∾

Trapped.

That was the only word that came to Maggie's mind as she frantically tried to figure a way out of the situation. She could either go back upstairs to the hotel room that her boss had reserved for the two of them—unbeknownst to her—or she could sleep on the street.

Martin Blake had been the model boss; for a year she'd been his executive assistant, and never in her wildest dreams could she have imagined that something like this would happen to her.

Maggie looked around the lobby—in search of what she didn't know. She had no money, no form of transportation, and no form of ID. Martin had seen to that. They were three thousand miles from home on the other side of the country. He was smart to choose now to hatch his disgusting plan. There actually was a conference going on, but Martin had very little interest in it; his focus was seducing Maggie.

She felt sick. At any moment, she was sure she was going to be ill. Collapsing on one of the opulent sofas in the hotel lobby, tears began to fall. "What am I going to do?" she cried gently, knowing that no one was there to answer her.

"Excuse me, miss," a gentle voice asked. "Are you okay?"

Tears streaming down her face, Maggie looked up and saw a man, probably in his late fifties, staring down at her, his face one of calm concern. Who was he? Did Martin send him to find her? Frantically, she looked around before turning her attention to him.

"I... I'm fine," she lied.

The man sat down at the opposite end of the sofa, not wanting to scare her more than she obviously was. "Are you sure? Is there someone I can call for you?"

The thing was, there wasn't anyone Maggie felt she could call about this situation. She didn't want to alarm her family; she had no close friends who could pay for a flight home for her—especially when she had no ID to present when she got to the airport. Shaking her head, a fresh wave of tears fell.

"Whatever it is, I'm sure it will be okay. Please, tell me what's going on? Do we need to call the hotel management? The police?"

As much as Maggie had wanted to say yes, Martin's taunting words came to mind. As she had been clawing to get out of the hotel room, he'd mocked, "Go ahead and call the cops or hotel security. I'll just tell them we had a lovers' spat and you are trying to blackmail the boss. I believe they call that extortion, and it's a crime, Mags."

"No!" she cried, coming back to the present. "No, please... no one needs to call the cops or security. I'll... I'll be fine."

The man looked at her with obvious disbelief. He had a briefcase at his feet and he reached for it, pulling it into his lap and opening it. Without a word, he handed her his card. "I'm William Montgomery. I'm from Charlotte, North Carolina. That's where my company is, too. It's been in my family for three generations and, God willing, it will go to my sons and they'll carry on long after I'm gone. I've got three sons; always wanted a daughter, though," he said lightly.

"I don't normally come to these conventions; seems like a great waste of time. Most of the attendees are here looking for a break from work, not to learn more about how to do their jobs more effectively." He sighed wearily and then smiled. "We drew straws, my sons and I, to see who would come and check this place out. I lost." He gave a light chuckle and felt relief when Maggie gave a small smile. "I'm too old for nonsense like this. Conventions are a young man's game."

William looked around the lobby, clearly unwilling to leave her in such distress.

"Although, most of the young men I met here today need to learn a lot more, not only about business, but about respect in general."

Maggie nodded and wiped at her tear streaked face.

William reached for a handkerchief in his pocket and handed it to her. "I don't know about you, but it certainly makes me lose a bit of faith in this generation."

"I agree," Maggie said softly.

William couldn't help but smile. He wanted so badly to help this woman, but she was clearly spooked. Something had happened and he may never find out exactly what it was, but he knew that he had to get her out of the hotel and to someplace where she'd feel safe.

William smiled at her. His manner was fatherly, caring, nothing at all like the way Martin had treated her. "Listen," he said calmly, "how about we go over and have a cup of coffee? The café over there is still open."

"Oh, I can't," she said nervously. "I don't have my wallet with me."

"It's my treat." When Maggie hesitated, William quickly added, "You'd be doing me a huge favor. I've done nothing today but talk to a bunch of upstarts with over-inflated egos."

Maggie thought about it for a moment and realized that

maybe it would be okay to join him for coffee. She hadn't had anything to eat since they'd left Virginia on the early morning flight, Martin hadn't allowed her to eat all day. Sadistic bastard.

She stood and said a quiet, "Thank you."

William towered over her petite frame. "It's my pleasure, Ms...." He left the words dangling.

"Maggie," she said finally. "Maggie Barrett."

"Well, it is a pleasure to meet you, Maggie Barrett," he said, his tone nothing but friendliness, and Maggie knew in that instant that things just might work out all right.

True to his word, William had set the wheels in motion to get Maggie settled into her new position. Within an hour, he had all her belongings transferred to the executive floor, and from where he stood in his office doorway, he could see her working with Rose. After lunch, they would sit down together with Jason and get things moving.

It did his heart good to see her up here working where she belonged. He hated pushing her into it, but deep down, William knew he'd let her hide out too long. What that bastard had done to her back in California so long ago had been traumatic for sure, but William also knew that Maggie had too much to give to spend her life hiding away from everything and everybody.

When William had offered her the position with Montgomery's, she been shocked and more than a little apprehensive. Desperate to help her when she was so clearly in need, he had vowed to meet her every wish in order to get her to agree to work for him.

She had wanted a low profile position; he gave her one.

She needed to get her belongings from where she lived in Virginia to North Carolina. William paid for the move and put her up temporarily in an executive apartment that the company owned until she found a place of her own.

He'd sent people to get her car and had taken care of ending her employment with Martin Blake without letting anyone within the man's company know where she was going.

William was very thorough in everything he did, and if keeping this woman under the radar for a little while meant keeping her safe, he'd do it.

Her final request was that no one know that she was single.

While William didn't think that would deter some men, he knew that no one within his company would dare approach Maggie in an unprofessional manner. So, he'd agreed to her request and no one was the wiser. Luckily, it wasn't something that came up very often. According to his human resources manager, Ann Kincade, Maggie was a virtual loner. She was pleasant to work with, but never engaged in any outside activities with her coworkers, mostly keeping to herself.

For a moment, William felt remorse at forcing her so clearly out of her comfort zone, but then he thought of how well it had worked last year when he'd done the same for his son Lucas, and silently prayed that he would have similar results.

Plus, the more he thought about it and with everything he knew about Maggie, he knew she'd be the perfect assistant for his son.

And...if he were truly being honest, he knew she'd be perfect for Jason, period.

"Only time will tell," he murmured as he smiled at Maggie.

Maggie sensed William's stare, looking up and giving him a weak smile. By now, she knew her boss could be trusted and was sure that his son would be no different. Still, she wasn't happy that this promotion, this shift in her life, was not her decision. Just like having to move her entire life from Virginia years ago. Although... she could say with great certainty that everything had worked out just fine with that.

To this day, she was still a little in awe of the fact that not only had every aspect of her move gone smoothly, but that he had somehow managed to get all of her personal belongings back from her former boss.

Was she lonely? Yes.

Did she miss some of her friends from back home? Yes.

Was she interested in making new friends here? Well... you'd think after three years that she would be, but she found it was hard to let her guard down with anyone.

It was a crappy way to live, but at least she wasn't forced to be looking over her shoulder every minute, wondering what was going to happen next.

For now, she would have to take William's word on this entire situation. After all, customer service was a bit mind-numbing and she used to enjoy a good challenge at work.

Just not the kind that would lead to being sexually assaulted by her boss.

Okay, that's not going to happen here...

For the last hour, Rose had been singing Jason's praises. He was a great boss, very fair, very focused, very respectful.

Basically, it sounded like the man was far more interested in the world of finance than he was in the opposite sex.

And that suited her just fine.

Plus, if Jason Montgomery was even remotely like his father, then she knew she could relax. At least a little.

From the moment she'd met him, William had been the epitome of a gentleman. From the respectful way he spoke to her, to his impeccable manners, she had a feeling he passed some of those qualities onto his sons. And even though she paid little attention to office gossip, she had to admit that she'd never heard any complaints about the Montgomery men, and certainly nothing that would even imply that any of them had acted inappropriately toward any of their employees.

It put her mildly at ease. Not that it mattered. This was happening and she would find a way to deal with it.

It was going to take a little while to adjust to it.

Working with Rose was no hardship; the woman knew her job and was easy to talk to. The job itself had some challenges that were actually related to her skills, but for the most part, the biggest challenge was going to be in relaxing and trusting the man she was going to assist.

Maggie had seen Jason Montgomery often enough around the building. He was certainly an attractive man and his mere presence seemed to bring out sighs from the women working around her. That always irritated Maggie. She would never show any outward signs of attraction to anyone. No matter how attractive that six-foot-tall, sandy haired, dark eyed package was!

Looking back, she knew that she had had no attraction to her former boss; she had genuinely liked Martin as a person. That was it. He was a good boss and a decent businessman, and she thought that was it. She'd respected him.

Somehow, however, he mistook that feeling for sexual interest, and thought that gave him the right to seduce her. Just
the thought of it now, years later, still made her sick to her
stomach.

"Are you okay?" Rose asked.

Shaking her head to clear it, Maggie looked at her.
"Sure. Why?"

"You just had a weird look on your face and you kind of
went pale." Rose looked at her watch. "Why don't we stop
here and break for lunch? I have you and Mr. Montgomery
scheduled to meet with Jason at two o'clock. You'll have an
hour for lunch and then about thirty minutes after you get
back to get organized and write up any questions you have
for him. Will that work?"

"Yes, thank you," Maggie said with a smile, relieved that
Rose didn't push her for more of an explanation.

In all the years since, no one knew the story of how she
had ended up working for Montgomery's. William had
been true to his word, and it wasn't something Maggie ever
wanted to talk about.

Walking to her desk, Maggie picked up her tablet and
satchel. Her plan was to start making notes now on the
things she wanted to discuss with Jason Montgomery. Natu-
rally, there would be the obvious ones: she needed to know
about this project and what all it entailed. She should have
asked his father about whether the position came with a pay
raise or paid time off.

Not that she ever took time off or went anywhere...

Once she stepped outside, she walked to the corner café
and found herself a quiet spot to sit. Normally, she packed
her lunch at home and ate at her desk, but today seemed
like a good day to get out of the office and clear her head a
bit. It was crazy how much she had missed doing this sort of

thing and hopefully she could make herself relax enough to do a bit more of it in the future.

After ordering a salad, Maggie pulled her tablet out of her satchel and began typing up the few questions she thought about on the ride over. She was very methodical and tried to think of all the pertinent things that would need to be covered.

The hour passed by quickly and by the time she walked back to the office, she couldn't say with any certainty that she was more prepared. She was still nervous, still not happy with this turn of events, but as she stepped onto the elevator, she decided on the very first thing she was going to ask Jason Montgomery.

"Are you someone who plans on mistaking a simple smile for an invitation to sexually harass me?"

TWO

"WHAT?"

"Is there a problem? I think the question was fairly simple."

Jason looked at the woman sitting across from him at the conference table and then at his father. "This is some sort of joke, right?"

"I'm the one speaking. If you have something to say, I would appreciate it if you would address me directly." Maggie looked at him, her brows furrowed. "And I don't think this is a joking matter, Mr. Montgomery. The question speaks for itself. Are you the kind of man who can tell the difference between someone being polite and someone offering an invitation?"

"What the hell kind of question is that?" he yelled and then turned to his father. "Seriously? This is who you think is the best option to work with me?"

William could barely contain his mirth. "She meets and actually exceeds all of your requirements, Jace. She's got the computer skills, organizational skills, and customer service skills that will prove useful for your trip, plus she has years of experience as an executive assistant."

Jason narrowed his eyes as he heard his father's words. "If she's so qualified, why has she been working in customer service all this time?"

Maggie had had enough. "Again, if you have a question about my qualifications, Mr. Montgomery, please address me. I am more than capable of answering *your* questions."

Jason couldn't help but note her obvious dig at his inability to answer her earlier question. "Fine," he bit out. "If you have all of these qualifications, why haven't you been assigned to anyone in all of your years with Montgomery's?"

"I was a bit burned out after my last assignment with my previous employer and wanted something a little less stressful."

"And you think now you're ready to handle the stress again?" he asked.

Her first response was to say no and hope that he'd let her leave and go back to her quiet position three floors down, but she knew she had made a promise to William. "Yes, I believe that I am more than capable of taking on this assignment. Your father has every confidence in me, and you should as well."

All he did was frown at first. "Ann tells me that you're married. How does your husband feel about you taking on a position that will have you traveling for the next several weeks?"

Maggie was not a very good liar, but said a silent prayer that she'd sound believable. "My husband travels a great deal for his job, so we both have no issues with this trip."

That sounded plausible, didn't it?

She looked over at William and saw his slight nod of approval.

Jason looked over Maggie's resume and personnel file. "This is not in any way, shape, or form a pleasure trip. We'll be working long hours and meeting with a lot of people. It is imperative that you be able to keep up the pace and keep notes on all of our dealings and get whatever information is needed back here to Rose for her to process. Is that going to be a problem?"

"I can assure you," Maggie began, "that I am highly organized and I don't have any issues with the long hours. It will be a refreshing change of pace after doing the eight-to-five schedule."

"We'll have no regulated schedule," Jason countered. "Some days we may be up at dawn for an early morning meeting, other days we may not be meeting with anyone until the late afternoon. When we're not in scheduled meetings, we'll be working together on organizing the data we've collected, planning ahead for our next clients, or traveling. Maybe all at one time. Will that be a problem?"

Maggie shook her head. "As I said, I believe I am more than up for the challenge."

"It won't leave you a lot of personal time. You'll be more than compensated for all the overtime and I will try to make sure that you're not overwhelmed, but I won't have time for someone who feels the need to make constant calls to home or has a jealous or needy spouse who needs to call you several times a day."

"That won't be a problem," Maggie said firmly.

"Be sure that it's not, Mrs. Barrett," Jason said with equal firmness.

"Ms.," she corrected. "I prefer to go by Ms. Barrett."

He arched a brow at her. Was this woman for real?

William chose that moment to interrupt. "I think the two of you have more than enough to get started on. I have some calls to make. Jason, why don't you take Maggie to your office and let her get started going over all the client files?"

Jason nodded and stood. Maggie did the same. "Maggie, if you have any questions, please feel free to come and see me, okay?" William said gently, his hand on her arm, and Jason had to wonder at the exchange. His father was notoriously kind to all of his employees, but he sensed that there was something different about the relationship between the two of them. He was about to comment on it when Maggie turned and headed for the door.

"Jason?" his father said quietly.

He saw that Maggie had exited the office, and he turned and looked at his father.

"Maggie is exactly what you're looking for. If you push, she's going to push back. You won't have to worry about her like you did with the others. She's going to do a good job for you on this trip."

At the moment, Jason wasn't so sure. While he could appreciate Maggie's credentials, he had a feeling that their personalities were going to clash, and that was almost as inappropriate as some of his former assistants' behavior.

Which is exactly what he said to his father.

"You need to trust me on this," William said. "Right now, I know it seems like Maggie's a little..."

"Antagonistic?" Jason supplied.

With a short laugh, his father shook his head. "Maggie Barrett is an incredibly intelligent woman who is going to be a great asset to you on this trip."

"It seemed like she was here under protest."

"Well..."

"Dad, what did you do?" he asked wearily.

"You were making demands on poor Ann and I stepped in to help." Pausing, he looked toward the door that Maggie had just exited through before looking at Jason again. "I know she is going to be the perfect fit for you. Her previous employer was... shall we say... difficult."

"What does that even mean?"

"It means it's not my place to discuss it," William said firmly. "All you need to know is that girl is a hard worker and once the two of you are done assessing one another, I believe everything will settle into place."

Jason wasn't quite so sure, but he trusted his father more than anyone else in the world.

"I hope so, Dad."

"But...?"

He chuckled because his father always seemed to know when there was more to say. "But," he went on, "I just... she seems almost... hostile. If she really doesn't want the position..."

"She does," William assured him and then he laughed softly.

"What? What's so funny?"

"I would think you'd appreciate the fact that she wasn't fawning all over you. After all, from everything you've been telling me and Ann, you need someone who is guaranteed not to look at you as marriage material. From what we just saw, I'd say we hit the nail right on the head."

He sighed, sliding his hands into his trouser pockets. "I suppose, but I don't want to spend all our time arguing either. There's a lot riding on this trip. It wouldn't look good for me, or Montgomery's, if I'm constantly arguing with my assistant."

"I don't believe that's going to be the case. Like I said,

once you and Maggie get to know one another a little, things will be fine."

He shrugged. "Maybe. I just need this trip to go smoothly. I've been working on it for so long and…"

"That's pressure you've put on yourself, Jace. You wanted to try for this expansion, and while I think it's a great idea, I don't want it to consume you to the point of pushing yourself so hard that you forget to live a little."

"What the hell does that mean?" Jason snapped.

"It means that you have a great work ethic and a desire to see the company succeed. Just don't forget that Montgomery's isn't your whole life." Smiling, he reached out and squeezed his son's shoulder. "At the end of the day, it's just a job. And if you don't stop and look around once in a while, the world and all its possibilities are going to pass you by."

Sometimes his father spoke like Yoda, and right now Jason didn't have the time to delve any deeper into what he was saying. He had to get Maggie acclimated to his project and make sure she was completely prepared when they left in two weeks for their whirlwind trip.

He just hoped they didn't strangle one another first.

Jason had done a damn good job. Sitting on the private plane that was getting ready to take off, he looked over at Maggie and smiled. They had worked long hours for the last two weeks, and she was just as familiar with every aspect of this project as he was. She was smart, inquisitive, and well versed. He knew without a doubt that she was going to be an asset to him on this trip and that he wouldn't have to spend precious time explaining things to her, because she clearly understood exactly what it was he was trying to accomplish.

Not once during the previous weeks had there been an issue with the long hours. At first, Jason was sure that her husband was going to put up a fight; after all, Maggie had been working fairly regular hours for so many years, so this was quite a change. But just as there'd been no complaint from the husband, Maggie hadn't complained either.

They'd worked side by side from eight in the morning until sometimes as late as ten at night. Jason found that after their initial clashing during their interview, they both seemed to come to understand one another and had formed a mutual respect for one another. Conversation flowed when it was needed and at the same time, they were both comfortable working in silence. For having worked together for only two weeks, they were seemingly in sync.

Jason wasn't used to that.

If anything, at least in the last few months, he had come to grips with his assistants wanting to talk about his personal life whenever there was a lull in the conversation. And even when they were strictly in work mode, he felt like he still had to prompt them with what they needed to be doing next.

That wasn't the case at all with Maggie.

And this is why I should never doubt my father...

"If we don't hit any delays, we should be in Chicago by ten. I called and confirmed the town car, and since we'll have missed most of the morning traffic, we should be at the hotel by eleven," Maggie was saying as she glanced at their schedule on her tablet. "We're meeting the Claremont people at one, so once we're checked in, we can have lunch brought up to the rooms and be ready to go by twelve thirty." She looked up at him. "How does that sound?"

"Good," Jason said distractedly. Meetings like this didn't normally stress him out, but this plan for expansion that he had made him a little edgy. "Did we leave the evening free, or did you pencil something in?"

"I left it free just in case they wanted to meet over dinner. I didn't want to over-schedule us on our first day," she said lightly. "I've researched several restaurants in the area, and the one at our hotel would actually be perfect for a meeting. I can call in a reservation now if you'd like, just in case?"

She was very efficient; that was what Jason admired most. Maggie was certainly making his life easier already. "Let's wait and see how the afternoon goes. For all we know, they can be exhausting and not people we want to work with. In which case, we'll just have a quiet dinner and discuss our next plan of attack."

Maggie laughed. "Sounds like a plan. I'll just mark these places for future reference."

While she was busy tapping away on her tablet screen, Jason studied her. With her blonde hair pulled back into a severe ponytail and her brown eyes downcast, she seemed to do her best not to stand out. Jason had to wonder a little about that. While he could appreciate her professional manner and her obvious desire not to draw attention to herself, he couldn't help but wonder why. Most of the women he knew, both in business and in his personal life, did things to make themselves look attractive. Maggie, on the other hand, wore little to no makeup, dressed ultra-conservatively, and did her best to blend into the back-ground. This was exactly what Jason had said that he wanted, but the more he got to know her, the more he had a feeling that she wasn't presenting her true self.

Their captain announced their turn for takeoff, and

Jason watched Maggie's response. Her white-knuckled grip on the seat told him that flying was definitely not her thing. While most of their travels were going to require flying, there were going to be some shorter legs that he had planned a rental car for. They hadn't discussed whether she had an aversion to flying. She knew the itinerary like the back of her hand, and she never once mentioned it. But seeing her reaction to take off right now, he was sure she would be relieved on the days they opted to drive.

"Not a fan of flying, huh?" he asked, hoping to distract her.

"No, not really."

"It's not so bad," he said in a soothing tone. "The key is to just relax."

"Easy for you to say," she mumbled, and heard Jason laugh.

"Look, don't focus on what you're feeling, focus on me."

Maggie's eyes went wide. "Excuse me?" she said, indignant.

He realized how that must have sounded and instantly put her mind at ease. "I mean, talk to me about this meeting today. Talk to me about the weather. Talk to me about what you think of my tie," he suggested.

"Your tie?"

"Sure. Whatever you need to talk about, we'll talk about," he said and smiled at her confused look. "So, what do you think? Stripes? Is it a good look? Should I have gone with a solid or something a little more muted?"

He was teasing her, and he knew the instant she relaxed. In their time working together, they had always kept things on a business level; they never talked about anything even remotely personal. But right now, he knew it would be beneficial to try to lighten the mood. The smile she gave him was a pleasant surprise. Her dark eyes twinkled, and it was good to see that he was helping.

"I'm not normally a fan of stripes," she said, her gaze lingering on his tie. "But they aren't overly obnoxious."

"Stripes are obnoxious?" he asked.

"They can be. Think of prison stripes."

That made Jason laugh again. "Well, I can guarantee you I will not be going for the prison stripe look. Ever."

"Good to know," Maggie said as she let out a long breath."

"Better?"

She nodded. "Definitely. For a minute there, my stomach was queasy and I was afraid I'd embarrass myself." She loosened her grip on her seat and looked out the window. "Is that it? We're done with takeoff?"

Jason smiled at her. "See? A little distraction always works." The next two hours passed quickly, and soon they were in the car and heading for their hotel. Check in went like clockwork. Jason was glad they had adjoining rooms. They were only going to be in Chicago for two days, but it would make things easier if Maggie was close by when he needed her help.

No sooner were they settled in their rooms than lunch was being delivered. While he had been checking them in, she had been taking care of ordering their food. Jason knocked on the door dividing their rooms and Maggie unlocked it and let him in.

"That was fast," she commented as she reached for her satchel.

Jason stopped her. "Whoa, lunch just arrived and we're going to eat lunch like normal people and not talk business for the next fifteen minutes, okay?"

She more than readily agreed. They had been talking

business for weeks and she felt like if Jason were to fall ill, she could handle any and all of his meetings because she knew the details so intimately. To have a few minutes' reprieve to eat and relax sounded like heaven.

Their lunch had been set up on the table in his room, and Jason waited for Maggie to sit down before joining her. "I hope you had enough time to get at least a little settled in your room."

Maggie waved him off. "I don't plan on getting too comfortable. It makes it easier when it's time to leave if I haven't taken everything out."

"That makes sense. Did you have time to call home?"

"What for?" she asked without thinking.

Jason arched a dark eyebrow at her. "I thought you would check in with your husband and let him know we arrived safely."

"Oh," Maggie said, forgetting for a moment that she was supposed to be married. "I texted him. He's at work, so I just figured we'd talk later tonight."

It sounded believable enough, but Jason had to wonder how good a marriage she had if they spent so much time apart and didn't seem to mind it at all. If he was married, he'd certainly be uncomfortable with his wife traveling with another man. What was wrong with her husband?

Why are you even complaining? This is exactly what you asked for. Stop looking for problems!

Clearing those thoughts from his mind, Jason took a bite of the BLT Maggie had ordered for him and then asked, "Have you ever been to Chicago before?"

She was delicately eating a chef's salad and held a finger up while she finished chewing before answering. "Actually, I haven't. It was never on my radar as someplace I wanted to see and I'm not really focusing on it now, since we're not here to sightsee."

Practical, Jason thought, and for just a minute he felt bad about not making any time to show her some of the sights. It seemed like she led a very quiet, sheltered life, and it made him a little sad for her. With a husband who seemed to lack any interest in her and her quiet acceptance of it all, it just didn't sit well with him.

Again, why are you even thinking about this? Who cares what her marriage is like? It's making your life so much easier. Stop looking for trouble!

"Are you a baseball fan?" he asked and she shook her head. "Oh, well, I thought maybe we could maybe find time to tour Wrigley Field, but if that's not something that interests you..."

Maggie gave Jason a serene smile. "I don't expect you to entertain me, Jason. We're here to make Montgomery's grow. That's not going to happen if we're off playing tourist."

While he should be happy that she wasn't looking for any personal attention from him, there was just something about her demeanor that was starting to get a little unsettling. He made another mental note to delve a little deeper into this as their trip went on.

"You're right about that," he finally answered. "I always tell myself that I'm going to take the time and go and see a game, but I never do. Are there any sports that you enjoy?"

"Hockey."

Jason almost choked on his sandwich. "*Hockey? Seriously?*"

Maggie looked at him with confusion. "What's wrong with hockey?"

"Nothing, nothing at all, it's just that I thought for sure you would have said something like tennis or golf."

She laughed out loud and Jason found that he enjoyed the sound of it. "Why on earth would you think that?"

"Well, for starters, you're a fairly conservative woman. Hockey is a loud, obnoxious, violent sport. I just can't see you standing up and screaming at a game."

"Well, believe me, I have done my share of screaming. I think hockey has got to be one of the most exciting and challenging sports there is to play. There's so much going on and it's just fascinating to watch."

"Who's your favorite team?"

"The Rangers."

"New York? You're a *New York* fan? Aren't you from Virginia?"

"What does that have to do with anything? Virginia doesn't have a hockey team and the Rangers are awesome!"

"How many games have you gone to?" he asked, still in disbelief that they were even having this conversation.

"Not nearly enough," she said lightly. "I've only gone to New York twice and I was a teenager. My dad took me to a game at Madison Square Garden and it was amazing. Then last year, I managed to go and see the Rangers play the Hurricanes in Raleigh."

"Is your husband a hockey fan, too?"

"What? I mean, yeah, sure. He's okay with it."

"Raleigh's not that far away. I'd think that you would try to go more often."

"It's three hours of driving each way. To go to a game would make it a two-day event and I just don't have that much time to invest, you know? Besides, there's something magical about seeing a team play on their home ice. The vibe at the Garden is completely different from what I felt in Raleigh."

Jason tucked that bit of information away as he glanced at his watch. "If we're going to get everything done, we need to finish up here. The car will be back for us in fifteen minutes. Will that be enough time for you?"

"I'm ready," Maggie said dismissively, pushing her unfinished salad aside. "All I need to do is grab my satchel. I've got everything we need for today in there, organized and ready to go."

Finishing his last bite of sandwich, Jason rose from his chair, went in search of his own briefcase, and then turned back to Maggie. "So, what do you think? Do I stick with the stripes or do I need to change?"

"Don't be such a diva, Jason," she said teasingly as she stood. "You look fine." She turned and walked into her room to grab her things, and Jason realized that her opinion really was beginning to matter.

And that could definitely be a problem.

It was well after eight when they were finally riding the elevator back to their floor at the hotel. Maggie leaned back against the wall and sighed. "I didn't think they'd ever stop asking questions. I mean, in every scenario I played out in my mind, none of them went like this."

Jason faced her as he leaned against the opposite wall. "I know what you mean. I think I sort of zoned out there after a while." He scrubbed a weary hand over his face and let his head fall back. "And as if that wasn't enough, what was with the dinner they brought in?"

"Oh, I know, right? I thought Chicago was known for its

good food! I have no idea where that stuff even came from. It seemed like someone made those sandwiches at home!" She laughed, but it was true. In all her years working in the corporate world, she'd never been served such an awful meal. It was like eating at the Fyre Festival.

"Want to order some real food for us, or do you want to go down to the restaurant to eat?" he asked.

"Honestly, I want to kick off these shoes and crawl into bed." Maggie stopped and considered what she was saying. "Okay, maybe I have the energy for some ice cream, but nothing more than that."

Jason chuckled. "I may order a pizza."

That piqued her interest. "Pizza? Well... I guess I could stay awake for some pizza."

"Atta girl," he said, still laughing. They arrived at their floor and headed for their rooms. "Why don't you go and relax and I'll call you when the pizza gets here."

"Bless you," Maggie said as she practically fell through her door. Within minutes, she had stripped out of her business attire that was beyond uncomfortable after such a long day and changed into a pair of yoga pants and a t-shirt. Certainly Jason didn't expect her to be dressed in her work clothes all the time, did he?

The only thing keeping her from completely relaxing was the fact that she had to keep her bra on. It was one thing to dress casually around Jason, it was another to go braless.

"Do I want pizza that bad?" she asked her reflection. There was always room service. It wouldn't necessarily be a bad thing for her to shoot Jason a text saying she'd changed her mind and was simply too tired, would it?

Unfortunately, pizza was one of her weaknesses and

she'd heard enough about Chicago's deep dish pizza that she was curious.

"Dammit."

She pulled the clip from her hair and massaged her scalp. Working longer hours was taking a little more getting used to. During her stint in customer service, her workday was relatively short compared to what she was doing now, and staying in such a severe look was getting uncomfortable. Staring at her reflection in the mirror, Maggie considered what else she could do with her hair to make it look professional without killing her scalp. Running her fingers through her long hair, she shook it out and found that she felt much better.

The thought of putting it back up, even in a less severe style was beyond unappealing. "Why am I even obsessing over this? It's hair, for crying out loud. If it freaks him out that much, then that's on him," she murmured, massaging her head a little more. "And if he wants to make some sort of inappropriate comment, then..." She sighed. "I can just kick him in the nuts and walk out."

Only... she knew that would never happen because it wasn't an issue.

As much as she hated to admit it, William Montgomery was right. Working with Jason was nothing like working with her previous boss. She and Jason definitely butted heads right at the beginning, but they settled into a routine and a working relationship based on respect and strong work ethics. He was brilliant at what he did, and she truly admired the fact that he was determined to take on a project like this and put himself out there to try to bring in new clients.

And on top of that, he was a gentleman.

Within minutes, she was almost feeling like her old self

and completely relaxed. She eyed the bed and wondered if she had enough time to just lie down for a few minutes. Deciding that she did, she laid down and let out a long breath. Reaching for her phone, she scrolled through the news app that she used and settled in to read. She had just gotten comfortable when Jason knocked on the door.

"Pizza delivery!"

Damn, so soon?

A quick glance at the bedside clock showed it was almost nine o'clock. Slowly, she got to her feet and stretched before shuffling over to the door. She opened it with a smile. "Do you want to eat in here, or are you already set up in your room?"

Jason couldn't speak. For a moment, he could only stare. The woman he had come to know these last weeks was gone, replaced by someone completely different. With her hair loose, he realized just how long it was. It was wavy and thick and wonderful, and he found himself itching to reach out and touch it to see if it was as soft as it looked. She had bangs that were wispy and light and seemed to drag his attention to her expressive brown eyes.

Eyes that were staring curiously at him right now.

Oh, right. Pizza.

"I've got everything set up inside," he said gruffly, and then turned back toward his room. "I had them send up some drinks, too. I wasn't sure what you wanted, so I got a variety."

"I probably shouldn't have anything with caffeine this late, but there is something to be said for a Coke with pizza."

"A girl after my own heart," he said and then realized how awkward that was. "What I mean is..."

Maggie laughed. "It's okay, Jason. I know what you meant." She sat down and helped herself to a slice of the deep dish pizza and groaned with delight at the first bite. "Now that is real food," she said with a sigh. "I can understand why they didn't order something like this for lunch, but I'm still stumped at those sandwiches they brought in for dinner." She took another bite and hummed happily.

Jason held in his own groan. With her new look and the near orgasmic sounds, she was making while eating, he was starting to sweat. She was his assistant and she was a married woman! He should not be noticing these things about her, and yet he couldn't seem to stop himself.

All this time he'd been obsessing about women, his assistants, being attracted to him that he never even considered the possibility of him being attracted to one of them. In all his years of working at Montgomerys, it had never happened.

It was awkward as hell that it was clearly happening now.

"Aren't you going to have any?" she finally asked, her brown eyes watching him curiously.

"What? Oh, yeah, sorry. I guess my mind is still on the bizarre meeting from today."

"Please, no more talk about business," she pleaded. "I think I'd just like to forget that today even happened."

"I couldn't agree more," he mumbled.

But... there didn't seem to be anything else for them to talk about at the moment, and he wasn't surprised when Maggie brought up their meeting again.

"So, does that mean Claremont is off the table for prospective clients?"

He nodded. "I don't think we could meet each other's needs. I'd rather cut my losses now and move on to what's next."

"I hate to say it, but I agree. I'll email Rose in the morning with an update. Our next appointment isn't until ten tomorrow, and then our flight to Ohio is after dinner."

"Okay."

She continued to eat, but seemed a bit more chatty than usual. "Are most potential clients like this? I realize I've never sat in on meetings like this before, but I guess I'm just curious if this was the norm."

"Um…" He wasn't sure where to look. If he looked right at her, he was certain she'd be able to tell something was wrong. So, he stared down at his pizza as he replied, "I thought you didn't want to talk about business?"

"I don't, but…"

"They're not usually like this," he blurted out and then took a giant bite of his dinner.

"Oh. Okay. Thanks," she said quietly.

Jason merely nodded again. He couldn't focus. He needed Maggie to finish her pizza and go to her own room. His mind was spinning in a dozen different directions, none of which were business related, and he needed to get his thoughts back on track.

What the hell is wrong with me?

He'd been working for his family since he was a teenager and he had never, ever!, had inappropriate thoughts about anyone he worked with. Even the women who were very brazen in what they could offer him, he was just never once tempted. But right now? If Maggie said or did anything that remotely showed she had an interest in him, he knew he'd act on it.

And that scared the hell out of him.

Terrified him, actually.

There was no way he could throw her out of the room, but there was also no way he could sit across from her and act casual. He needed to put a little distance between them for tonight. Glancing around, he knew what he needed to do and hoped it wouldn't make him look like too big of an ass. His parents raised him to have good manners and right now, he was going to throw some of them right out the window.

Knowing he was being rude, Jason grabbed up another slice and stalked over to the other side of the room, sitting down with his laptop and doing his best to ignore her. "I just remembered some emails I need to respond to," he murmured without looking at her and prayed she'd get the hint and leave.

Within minutes, she did.

With a quiet "thanks for dinner," she closed the door between their rooms and Jason heard the lock go into place. That's when he let himself breathe again. If this was how he felt after one day, how the hell was he going to survive for another twenty?

He scrolled through his emails, but there was nothing that needed his attention.

Then he checked the news and some stocks and even got desperate enough to scroll through Facebook to see what kind of nonsense he could distract himself with.

And he definitely needed a distraction.

Hell, he needed someone to talk to, but there was no way he could call his father or even his brothers and tell them about this. No doubt his brothers would mock him and his father would be disappointed, so... that wasn't an option.

Taking a minute, Jason did his best to just try to think about this logically.

Maggie was an attractive woman. That much was obvious. But that didn't mean he was attracted to her, right? It was possible to find someone attractive without actually being attracted to them.

That was plausible, wasn't it?

And as for how he felt tonight, it was probably just a shock to see her looking so different. Again, shock did not equal being attracted to her.

"And I'm tired," he told himself. It was possible that his thinking was just slightly askew because he was exhausted. It had been a long day and he'd been on the go since the sun came up, so... there was that. No doubt tomorrow morning he'd meet Maggie out in the hallway and feel absolutely nothing for her.

Closing his eyes, the image of her sitting across from him with her hair down, smiling and laughing came to mind. With a groan, he forced himself to open his eyes, sit up, and finish his dinner while prepping for tomorrow's meeting.

He needed to keep his focus.

This trip had the potential to be a huge coup for him, and the last thing he needed was a distraction.

No matter how attractive it was.

THREE

THEY WERE airborne once again the following evening, and Maggie could tell that Jason wasn't pleased with their trip so far. Neither meeting had gone as expected, and she seriously hoped that he would not let this get him down.

"Well, tomorrow's another day," she said to break the silence.

He merely grunted in response.

"And the food was definitely better today," she went on. "I have to admit, I was a little leery when they mentioned bringing stuff in."

Another grunt.

She decided to make one last attempt to draw him out. "Neither of them was what Montgomery's is looking for. I'm glad we got them out of the way early and now we can move on to something better. Things can only get better, right?"

This time, he glared at her.

Okay, now what?

"I've been doing some research on our group for tomorrow. They have a similar history to Montgomery's, and Nick Austin, their CEO, is a huge football fan. I bet we can spend some time talking about Lucas to break the ice a little."

"I'm not using my brother's former career to schmooze anyone," he snapped. "That is not the way I do business."

"It was just a suggestion to..."

"We're not doing it," he quickly interrupted. "I refuse to look desperate by going in there and trying to wow him by telling second-hand stories about Lucas' career. And I don't appreciate you thinking that I don't know how to handle client meetings!"

That was it, she'd had enough.

"Look, I get that you're not happy right now with the way things have gone so far, but none of it is my fault. I didn't research the people to meet with, *you* did. I came into this whole thing late in the game and I don't appreciate having you snap at me for things that aren't my fault or for trying to make suggestions!"

"Maggie..."

"No," she said angrily. "I never once said that I didn't think you knew how to handle clients, I was simply offering a suggestion so we didn't walk in and immediately start talking business. You aren't big on small talk and I thought you might try it. Excuse me for trying to make you look like a decent guy rather than some sort of corporate robot!"

"Oh, so now I'm a robot? Seriously?" he countered, leaning forward in his seat. "Do you think telling me this is even remotely helpful?"

"You know what, Jason? I don't think anything would be helpful right now because you're angry and you want to stay angry. Forgive me for trying to lighten the mood a damn bit."

And with that, she snapped shut the book she was reading and turned to look out at the sun setting in the sky. The view was spectacular, but it did little to ease the tension she was feeling right now at Jason's miserable attitude.

She understood the reasoning behind it, but in the last several weeks, she'd never seen this side of him and right now he reminded her of a pouting child. They were only two days into this trip, and she wasn't sure she'd be able to handle working with him if this was how he was going to react when things didn't go his way.

Making a mental note to reach out to Rose and William tomorrow, she knew that was all she could do. As much as she hated feeling like she was tattling on him, there was no way she would last another two weeks dealing with his foul mood.

That part she'd be sure to only share with his father. Although... that definitely made it feel like she was looking to get him in trouble.

And maybe... she kind of was.

After she'd gotten over her initial reluctance, she'd been happy about the new position and all the challenges of being back in a department where she was really using her brain.

The challenge of a moody boss, however, was not what she signed on for. So, for the rest of this particular leg of the trip, she was going to simply keep her mouth shut and do her best to ignore him.

Ugh... why are men such babies?

Jason knew he was being a jerk and it wasn't fair to be taking out his anger on Maggie, but he was beyond frustrated. Between the miserable meeting yesterday, and the confusing way she'd made him feel last night, the very last thing he'd needed was another round of miserable meetings today. So far, this trip was a complete disaster and it had only just begun.

Not wanting to alert his father to the problem that was brewing, he'd had asked Maggie to wait before sending anything into the office. While he could tell she wasn't in complete agreement with him, she'd done as he asked and merely saved the information on her computer until he wanted it sent.

How about never, he thought to himself.

They would be landing late in Cleveland and Jason knew there'd be a town car waiting to take them to their hotel. By now, all he wanted was to be alone. His tie was choking him, his head was pounding, and he had no desire to make small talk anymore. Tomorrow would be here soon enough; they'd have to go back into schmoozing mode and do their best to kiss up to another group of potential clients that might be worse than what they'd dealt with in Chicago.

Maggie stayed silent for the rest of the flight and during the ride to the hotel. When Jason handed her the key to her room, she took it and quietly followed him into the elevator. She wouldn't even look at him and he knew he needed to say something to break the tension between them, because it certainly wasn't helping anything.

"Look, Maggie, I'm sorry I snapped at you earlier. I know none of this is your fault. I just had so much hope for this trip and I really thought I'd done thorough research on the people we were going to meet with." He let out a mirthless laugh. "I was so damn sure I'd gotten it all right, but none of it is going like I planned."

"It's okay, Jason," she said meekly, studying her room key. "I know you have a lot on your mind. You don't need to add worrying about me to the list."

"Dammit, that's not what I'm saying!" he yelled and then caught himself. Raking a hand through his hair, he wanted to pace but there wasn't enough room in the elevator. Plus, he needed to vent to someone and as well as they had been getting along, he didn't feel it was right for him to unload all his frustration on her. With a weary sigh, he said, "Let's just meet up in the morning down in the restaurant for breakfast. Maybe a good night's sleep will help."

They stepped off the elevator and Jason noted that this time Maggie's room was across the hall from him. "Good night," she said softly, her eyes still not meeting his, and he felt ten kinds of crappy.

No doubt she was going to go inside, lock the door, call her husband and tell him what a colossal jackass she was working with.

And it was no more than he deserved.

Unfortunately, between not being able to call his father or either of his brother's, he was a little at his wits end. After yanking his tie off and stripping down to his boxers, he couldn't relax. He'd paced, channel surfed, checked emails, read the news, and checked the sports scores.

And still, he couldn't relax.

Groaning, he walked over to the mini-bar and pulled out a bottle of water, but what he really needed was something stronger. After taking a long drink, he gave up the fight and called for room service and ordered himself a scotch and soda. He wasn't much of a drinker, but tonight it felt like the only solution to help him unwind so he could sleep.

Thinking about Maggie, he wondered if she was still going to be pissed at him in the morning or if venting to her husband helped her clear her mind.

"I wish I had someone like that," he murmured before he realized what he'd said.

What the hell is wrong with me? When did I get this needy?

Before he could even begin to analyze that, he realized he would need to put pants on, or a robe at least, before a server delivered his drink.

And maybe if it was strong enough, he wouldn't have to think about all the ways his life was becoming a bit of a shit show.

~

"A new day. New possibilities."

She had to admit, a good night's sleep seemed to help. But then again, she hadn't spoken to Jason yet. For all Maggie knew, her good mood was going to be shot right to hell before her first cup of coffee.

"Should have just made myself a cup up in the room," she murmured as she rode down in the elevator by herself.

They met up at eight in the restaurant, and Jason took great care to be fastidiously polite. He held her chair for her, asked how she slept, what she wanted to order, did she want anything special. By the time he unfolded her napkin for her, she was ready to scream.

"Okay, enough!" she said and almost laughed at his shocked expression. "Look, we were both on edge last night, but today is another day. Not all of these meetings are going to garner the results we want, but we can't let it freak us out. We've got another two and a half weeks to get through and we'll never make it if we get into a funk every time things don't go our way."

Jason took a deep breath and then seemed to relax. "You're right. I know you're right. I'm just a damn perfectionist and it's been a long time since things didn't go exactly as I had planned. I worked so hard on this and spent months working out every tiny detail. I guess I wasn't being particularly reasonable in my expectations."

She reached out, placed her hand on his, and then gasped softly when she realized what she'd done. Before she could pull her hand away, Jason's eyes met hers. Had he felt it too? It was like a spark, a warmth that wasn't there before and now suddenly was.

So not the time to be noticing things like this...

"Um, you shouldn't be so hard on yourself. I'm sure there are going to be a lot more successes than disappointments on this trip. You can't take it personally."

Then, slowly pulling her hand away, Maggie scanned the room for their server and prayed their food would arrive quickly. She needed the distraction.

Now.

"Did you tell your husband what a jerk I was?" he asked sheepishly.

Honestly, she didn't want to talk about the man she was fictionally married to, but maybe he needed to remind her of the fact that she was married. Especially after whatever has just passed between them.

"You weren't a jerk, Jason," she said kindly. "You were disappointed."

"That doesn't answer my question," he returned. "Did you tell him?"

"Um... it really didn't come up," she said, averting her eyes.

Luckily their food arrived and she put all her attention

on that. Her eggs were prepared over-easy and looked perfect, and so did the crispy bacon and home fries. It had been a struggle to decide between indulging in a not-so-healthy breakfast or going for a yogurt parfait.

Ultimately, the need for something yummy won out and now she was so glad it did.

"I have to admit, I don't normally indulge in a big breakfast, but sometimes it's a real treat."

Jason nodded. "I don't normally eat a large breakfast either, but when I'm on the road, I try to just in case I end up missing lunch because of a meeting. Back at home, if we're deep in work mode, Rose makes sure that food comes in. I can't guarantee the same thing when I'm relying on somebody else's timetable."

"I can only hope we have no more mishaps like that meal at Claremont's. I think I'd rather skip eating all together than have to eat food like that again."

Jason agreed.

Within an hour, they were climbing into their rideshare and heading to their first meeting of the day. "Remind me again how tight a schedule we're on today?"

Maggie pulled out her tablet. "Okay, we've got a ten a.m. with Nick Austin, a one o'clock lunch meeting with the Smith Group, and then we have to head back to the hotel and change because we've got the charity auction at the Rock and Roll Hall of Fame. I've got your tux and my gown with the concierge to be pressed and ready to go. We have a limo picking us up at seven, so we should have plenty of time after lunch to go over the two meetings and get a little time to relax before heading out for the night."

Jason was exhausted just thinking about it. "I really packed the schedule, didn't I?"

Maggie laughed. "Just a little."

"If it had been you doing all the planning, what would you have done differently?"

"So far?"

That didn't sound good. "With the whole trip," he answered.

"Well, I understand you're trying to maximize your time and really, you've done that with military precision."

"But..."

"But," she chimed in, "you didn't leave a lot of time for incidentals."

"Like what?"

"Well, let's say that this meeting with Nick Austin is going well and we need more time with him. We don't really have it because three hours after the start of our meeting, we're due to start another one. I would make sure that we worked in four-hour time blocks, nothing less."

"Okay," he said slowly. "How often do I give us less than four hours?"

Maggie scrolled through their itinerary and frowned. "Quite often. You have several appointments right on top of each other, and then other times you have up to eight hours between appointments. I realize sometimes that's all that is available, but it is going to have us in and out of the car a lot more than is effective."

"I didn't even think to look at it that way. I was more concerned with getting the appointments made than thinking about how efficiently I was spending my time." His tone was slightly defensive and he hated feeling like he'd made a mistake.

"It's okay, Jason. This was something you needed an assistant for. It's all going to work out just fine; some days it will seem like an adventure," she teased.

"I don't think I've ever looked at meetings quite that

way." He frowned. "Do you think we can try to make some calls and maybe rearrange some of the appointments?"

"Hmm..." she began and then paused. "Personally, I don't think it's necessary. We need to go with what you have planned and learn from it all for the next time."

He let out a low laugh. "Next time? I'm not sure we'll survive this." Shaking his head, he said, "The next time I come up with an idea like this, promise you'll talk me out of it."

"Jason, you're being too hard on yourself. And it's too early in the trip to just assume we're not going to survive or that it's all going to be bad. Just... have a little faith."

Easier said than done, he thought.

They pulled up to their first appointment and Maggie gave him a beaming smile. "Ready?" she asked.

"As I'll ever be," he said as he exited the vehicle.

They arrived back at the hotel at three thirty and Maggie already felt as if she'd run a marathon. The first meeting had gone extremely well, and their lunch meeting was pleasant enough, but the client was going to require a little more time before he signed any contracts with Montgomery's. All in all, she was pleased and knew Jason was too.

"I'll call the concierge and make sure our clothes are back up to us by six," she said as they walked toward their rooms. "Is there anything else you need before then?"

"I think we're good for now. What are you going to do with yourself this afternoon?"

Maggie thought for a moment. "Well, since there isn't much for me to do with the files for today, I'm going to send what I have to Rose and then maybe grab a nap, then take my time getting ready for tonight. What about you?"

"I've got some files I want to look over and a little research I want to do, but a nap certainly sounds appealing."

Smiling, Maggie took out her key card, turning toward her door.

"Listen," Jason said suddenly. "Why don't you make an appointment with the hotel salon and go and get pampered for tonight?"

Maggie looked at him as if he'd lost his mind. "Excuse me?"

He nodded. "You've been putting in some long hours and have had to deal with an extremely grumpy boss, so why don't you take a little time for yourself?" His words were spoken lightly. "Company treat!"

The thought was both appealing and unnerving at the same time. Was this how it was going to start? Was Jason going to woo her with spa treatments and special favors in hopes that she would feel indebted to him? The thought made her frown, but when she looked up at his face, which looked genuine and sincere, she knew he was nothing like her former boss.

"Are you sure?" she asked hesitantly.

"Of course I am," he said. "You've got nothing to do for a couple of hours, so call down and see if they have an appointment and do whatever it is that women do before they have to go to some formal charity event."

She laughed. "Honestly, I have no idea what that is! I've never gone to one before."

"Seriously? I would've thought that with your previous employer or even with your husband that you would have done something similar at some point."

At the mention of both the fake husband and her disgusting ex-boss, Maggie's stomach turned. Jason saw the look on her face and instantly stepped forward, concerned. "Maggie? Are you okay?"

"I'm fine," she quietly lied. "Let me see if they can squeeze me in for something." She opened her door and then turned back to Jason, her expression guarded and her tone stiff and formal. "Thank you. I appreciate your generosity."

As the door closed, Jason wondered, not for the first time, just what went on in her mind. There were times she was outgoing and friendly and seemingly full of joy, but it didn't take much to make her completely shut that side down. He was getting a little tired of not knowing what the trigger was, but he had a sinking sensation that it had to do with her marriage.

And that thought bothered him more than he was willing to admit.

Should he call his father and ask? After all, it seemed like the two of them knew each other rather well. Would it be the worst thing in the world for him to simply inquire about the best way to handle his new assistant so he didn't upset or offend her?

Sadly, the answer was yes.

If there was something she wanted him to know about herself, she would have told him. It would be wrong for him to go behind her back like that.

Even if it would make his life a hell of a lot easier.

At six forty-five, Jason knocked on Maggie's door. His tux had arrived promptly at six o'clock and he was dressed by six fifteen, so he found himself just pacing in his room with nothing to do. The limo would be downstairs in five minutes, and he hoped she would be punctual. He knew her to be so when it was for work, but most women Jason knew tended to take a lot longer to get ready when it was for a social event.

When she opened the door, Jason felt his jaw drop. She was stunning. In a navy blue strapless evening gown that hugged her petite, curvy body, she took his breath away.

"I wasn't sure quite how formal I needed to be," Maggie said as she tried to read Jason's expression. "I thought this was understated enough to be formal and classy."

He didn't say a word to either confirm or deny if she was right.

If anything, he just stared at her. But not in a creepy way. Still, she'd been so wrapped up in all the other details for the trip that formal wear sort of wasn't on her radar.

Why didn't I ask him this when I went shopping? Why wait until now to ask if it's okay? And what if it's not? Does that mean I don't get to go to the event? Would he really ask me to stay behind because of a dress? It would really stink if after an afternoon of pampering that I'd have to order crappy room service.

She wished Jason would say something, anything.

When they had originally discussed this event, all Jason had told her was to bring "some sort of gown." That wasn't much to go on. Maggie had researched previous events for this particular charity and then had done some major damage with her Visa card. The gown was a knockoff of a Christian Dior gown that some actress had worn to the Screen Actors Guild Awards, and though she normally didn't go for such a bold and sexy look, she had simply fallen in love with it.

Down at the spa, she had gotten a manicure, pedicure, and facial before getting her hair done. Gone was the severe ponytail of the workday, and in its place was an elegant chignon with a few loose tendrils that curled along the side of her face. All in all, she had been pleased with the look, but Jason's hard stare had her second-guessing herself.

"Jason?" she finally asked. "Are you okay? Did I get this all wrong?" Glancing down at herself, she frowned. "I didn't bring anything else, but..."

He quickly shook his head as if to clear it and then cleared his throat. "Yes, I'm fine, sorry. You look lovely. The gown is... it's perfect." He paused and seemed to realize what he'd said. "What I meant was..."

"Jason?" she quickly interrupted. "I know what you meant. It's fine."

"Oh. Okay. Good. Are you ready?"

It was the first real compliment Maggie had received from a man in over three years and it made her blush. She ducked her head slightly as she turned and shut the door, then managed to walk a few steps ahead of Jason to the elevators. They rode down in silence, and Maggie felt a twinge of excitement at the thought of the stretch limo waiting for them.

She turned an inquisitive eye to Jason. "Tell me again why we needed a limo?"

He smiled. "This is a big event," he said simply. "It required a limo."

Whether or not that was true, she didn't know, but in that moment, she realized how big a difference there was between her regular, ordinary life and the life of the wealthy Montgomerys. She felt a little inferior, but knew that was of her own doing. The Montgomerys never flaunted their wealth or their position and, if anything, they were beyond generous. For this one night, she was going to enjoy seeing how the other half lived and pretend it was nothing out of the ordinary for her.

That thought lasted until they pulled up to the venue and she found herself more than a little starstruck by the crowd. Rock stars, athletes, A-list celebrities milled about, and she almost had to pinch herself that she was actually going to be a part of this. As they made their way up the red carpet, Jason stopped and shook hands with many people, always introducing her, but after a few minutes, he stopped and pulled her over to the side.

"I know this is a little overwhelming, but you have nothing to be so nervous about," he whispered in her ear, and felt Maggie shiver.

"I'm not nervous," she lied, and then heard him chuckle as he seemed to pull her a little closer.

"You're practically glued to my side, Maggie. I can feel you shaking, and I can hear it in your voice every time you speak. Take a deep breath and relax, okay?"

She lifted her eyes to his and nodded. "Sorry. I guess I wasn't expecting such a star-studded event. I'm not sure who I thought would be attending, but... this wasn't it."

His smile was downright charming. "I probably should have warned you a little about that. You didn't strike me as the type to get starstruck."

Honestly, she wasn't sure if that was a compliment or an insult.

"Actually, I had no idea if I was the type because I've never been around any celebrities. I don't think I've ever even seen any from a distance." She paused. "Well... athletes. Hockey players. But that was to watch them play, not to hang out and socialize with them. I know that's completely different and... and I'm rambling. Sorry."

She went to hang her head and found that practically had it on his shoulder. They were standing way too close; she was plastered to him, but not in an uncomfortable way. It had been a long time since she had let any man get this close to her physically, and she found that with Jason, she didn't mind it all.

Warning bells went off in her head because now was so not the time for her to get comfortable in a situation like this. How ironic would it be after all these years of hiding away and all her conversations with Mr. Montgomery that she'd find herself developing feelings for Jason?

No. Absolutely not. It's just... you're caught up in the moment. This is a little like playing at being Cinderella, so... stop romanticizing it. Jason Montgomery is not your Prince Charming and you don't even want a Prince Charming, so... just stop it!

His dark gaze was burning into hers and Maggie licked her dry lips, forcing herself to take a small step back and look away. "So," she said, expelling the breath she had been holding and forcing a smile. "Are we ready to head in?"

Honestly, Jason needed another moment before he felt he was truly in control of his thoughts, but he didn't want to scare her. He simply nodded and took her hand, leading her up to the main doorway. It didn't even occur to him how that one single move might be inappropriate, and Maggie didn't pull away, but... he had to wonder at what in the hell he was thinking. He'd never held any of his former assistants' hands. Why now? Why her?

They stepped inside and he casually let go of her hand. Soon they were swept into the crowd and drinking champagne, Jason doing his best to meet up with the people that he wanted to while keeping track of Maggie at his side. They sat down for dinner, and he managed to make some new contacts. Glancing over, he caught her typing something into her phone and wondered if she was texting her husband. Looking up, she caught his gaze and smiled.

"Just making some notes," she whispered, and Jason instantly relaxed again. Maggie was savvy enough to put all of their information into her iPhone for future reference without being overly obvious about it.

Once dinner was over, the actual charity event presentation began. There were several performances by some big name artists in the music industry, and then the actor who had organized the event gave a twenty minute speech imploring the guests for their support. By ten o'clock, everyone was back to mingling, and Jason caught Maggie watching the couples dancing with a wistful look on her face.

He was deep in conversation with Brandon Wolfe, a young, self-made millionaire in video game design. Jason had never been much of a gamer, but it was still fascinating to hear how Brandon had used a Kickstarter campaign to raise money and now was the head of a very successful company. His gaze, however, kept going back to Maggie. She swayed a bit to the music as she slowly sipped her champagne, and he was just...drawn to her. There was no other way to describe it.

Fortunately, someone came over to speak to Brandon and Jason took that as his cue to make his way across the room. Unable to help himself, he placed his champagne glass down on the nearest table and intently walked toward her. At his approach, he asked, "Would you like to dance?"

Her eyes went wide with delight at first, but then she

seemed to school her expression as she looked around. "Are you sure? Don't you have more people to talk with?"

"I think I've done more than my share of talking tonight and even came out a little ahead. Besides, what kind of man would I be if I didn't make time to ask a beautiful girl to dance?"

Her eyes went even wider than they had a moment ago, even as she hesitated. He thought she was beautiful? This was probably all kinds of against the rules, slow dancing with her boss, but right now, it was all that she wanted to do.

Another downside to her self-imposed exile, she missed the simple act of human contact.

"What do you say, Maggie?" Jason asked again when she didn't respond to his initial request.

"I would love to," she said, placing her hand in his. There was that same jolt she'd felt when they touched at breakfast, but it didn't scare her this time; instead, she embraced it.

They joined the couples out on the floor and simply swayed to the orchestra. "I can't even remember the last time I went dancing," Maggie said as she aligned herself with Jason. "It may have been my senior prom." Then she giggled quietly. "Of course, that was a small-town high school gymnasium with a DJ and not a celebrity filled event with music by the New York Philharmonic." Looking up at him, she smiled. "So yeah, it's been a long time."

All sorts of thoughts raced through Jason's head. What about her wedding? Her honeymoon? Wasn't that the sort of thing couples did? He thought of his brother Lucas and his new bride Emma and the way they had danced at their engagement party and wedding. Hell, Jason may not be an expert on married couples, but he sure as hell knew that they danced! He was just about to make a comment on it when he felt Maggie snuggle a bit closer and sigh.

His body was on high alert. She felt very good in his arms, and without conscious thought, he wrapped his arm around her to pull her even closer, surprised when she didn't resist. Jason rested his head on top of hers and simply enjoyed the feel of her, the smell of her, the way her hair tickled his chin.

He was treading into dangerous territory here and yet couldn't seem to find the will to care. Luckily the orchestra moved smoothly into another slow song and he was treated to having Maggie close for another few minutes. Then what? The smart thing to do would be to thank her for the dance and then find a colleague or two to talk to, but that thought left him cold.

For several minutes, he tried to focus on something, anything, except the woman in his arms. He thought of her initial question to him during their interview and wondered if this was some kind of test. Maybe not a conscious one, but...

No. Maggie wasn't like that. He knew that it was just that his emotions were all over the place right now and he was confused because he was so turned on when he shouldn't be.

Maggie Barrett was his assistant.

His *married* assistant.

Even over the music, he heard her soft hum as she pressed even closer to him. Was she even aware of it? Was it... was it possible that she was attracted to him too?

Jason knew what he wanted, knew what he *needed*, knew without a doubt that it would be a mistake, and still couldn't bring himself to care. This was one of those rare moments where you had to either take a risk or spend the rest of your life regretting that you didn't. And there wasn't a doubt in his mind that he would regret it if he let this moment pass without knowing for sure if Maggie was attracted to him.

Lifting his head, he reached up and placed a finger under Maggie's chin so that her eyes met his. Her sexy, slumberous expression matched his own and he cursed himself as he lowered his lips to hers.

FOUR

THE MOMENT JASON'S lips touched Maggie's, he knew he was in trouble. It was perfect. He felt her slight tremble before she lifted her arms around his neck to pull him in closer. Jason wanted to devour her right then and there, but kept his touch soft and gentle so that if she wanted to pull away, she could.

But she didn't.

If anything, she seemed to do her best to drag a deeper kiss out of him. She was warm and curvy and everything he should stay away from, but couldn't. He heard another soft hum right before her hand raked up into his hair. She was drawing him in deeper and deeper. It would be easy to take this to the next level. To let his tongue tangle with hers as he let his hands roam over her magnificent curves.

He wanted to give in, he really did, but this was not the place. With a growl of regret, he raised his head, his breathing ragged. "Maggie?"

Slowly she opened her eyes and then he watched as reality slowly set in, shock and embarrassment crossing her face. *"Ohmygod,"* she blurted out in a horrified whisper, and ran from his embrace.

Jason stood motionless for a moment, not sure what he was supposed to do. Why had he given in to temptation? He was stronger than that! They had more than two weeks to go on this trip and he could *not* afford to screw this up and scare Maggie off. Not only that, he'd just crossed the line into some seriously dangerous territory as her boss.

Dammit!

Looking around, he noticed that no one was paying any attention to him, so he made his way off the dance floor, careful not to meet anyone's gaze, and went in search of his assistant.

It didn't take long to find her.

Her back was to him and even from across the room, he could see her trembling. His first instinct was to comfort her, but... he had a feeling that would only lead to more trouble. For all his talk about not wanting an assistant who crossed lines and acted inappropriately, he'd gone and done all of that himself.

I loathe myself...

Standing in the far corner of the lobby, Maggie tried to catch her breath. Dear lord, what had she done? She'd kissed Jason! She'd kissed her boss! What was she supposed to do now? Her mind raced frantically and her first instinct was to call William and tell him that she needed to leave immediately. She could be packed up and at the airport in no time, but it was already too late to get a flight home tonight. First thing tomorrow, however, it could happen.

But once she took a moment to think all that through, she realized *she* was the one who was at fault here, not Jason. Maybe she had misread his intentions? No, he was definitely the one who initiated the kiss, but she was the one who had practically devoured him.

Oh, God, am I that starved for affection that I have no common sense anymore?

She knew this assignment was a mistake. She knew she should have held her ground and said no to it, even if it meant losing her job. After carrying on about how she didn't want to be in the kind of position she'd found herself in years ago, she went and did something equally reprehensible.

Okay, calm down. It wasn't exactly like Jason was fighting you off...

While that was true, it the whole thing left her feeling dirty and more than a little humiliated.

Maggie was sure her face was twenty-seven shades of red and almost jumped out of her skin when she heard Jason say her name softly from behind her. Reluctantly, she turned to face him.

Before he could even say a word, she held up a hand to stop him. "That was completely unprofessional of me and I don't know why it happened." When Jason tried to speak again, she continued on. "Let's just say that I got a little swept up in the moment and it won't happen again. I completely understand that I was out of line and this was the exact sort of thing you were trying to avoid when you took me on as an assistant. I wouldn't blame you one bit if you reached out to human resources and filed a complaint."

"Maggie..." he began.

"Honestly, Jason, I'd rather not talk about it. I'm mortified at my behavior and... please." Fidgeting with hair, she reluctantly met his gaze. "If it's alright with you, I'll call for an Uber or something and head back to the hotel."

"You don't have to leave and you certainly don't have to call for an Uber."

She looked around the lobby and noticed that people were starting to leave. "Are there more people that you needed to talk to, or would you mind if we called for the car?"

Jason stared down at her skeptically. There were a million thoughts racing through his head. Caught up in the moment? That's all it was to her? *Hell no!* There was more to this than she was letting on, but the harder he stared at her, the more her bravado seemed to be failing and he felt like he was wordlessly bullying her. "No," he said finally. "I think it's been a successful evening. I'll call for the car."

Within twenty minutes, they were back in the limo and on their way to the hotel. Maggie sat as far away from him as she possibly could. She was going to try for small talk, but couldn't seem to find anything to talk about. They were going to be leaving Cleveland in the morning and had a flight to Boston. Their itinerary had them spending three days there and then they were heading to Manhattan for four days.

Right now, all she wanted was a day to herself to figure out what in the world was going on with her. She had been so confident in her ability to stay in control after the way things had gone down with Martin Blake that she never gave a thought to what would happen if she were the one attracted to her boss.

I'm no better than all those women he was trying to avoid...

She thought those feelings were long dead, ruined by a man who trapped her like some sort of prey. For some reason, Jason Montgomery was bringing feelings out in her that she wasn't ready to deal with. Being in such close proximity to him was certainly not helping the situation.

A cry of relief nearly escaped her lips when they finally arrived back at the hotel. Maggie noticed once they were in the lobby that Jason wasn't behind her. She stopped, turned, and saw him standing still, watching her. "Jason?"

"You go on up. I'm going to go grab a drink in the bar." He motioned to the hotel lounge behind him. "Why don't we plan on meeting down here to grab the car for the airport in the morning?"

"That sounds fine," she said quietly, knowing that Jason was probably trying to figure out how to get rid of her for the rest of the trip. "I'll see you in the morning." With that, she walked quickly and got on the elevator just as the doors were closing.

Jason was a wreck. Three shots later and nothing was making sense. He gave a mirthless laugh as he paid the bar tab and made his way to the bank of elevators. Why did he think more alcohol was going to help clear his mind? He wasn't a drinker. Not really. And not once in his life had he turned to alcohol for help. It just went to show how poor his judgment was.

Maggie had given him hell from the get-go about not mistaking a smile for a come-on. He could live with that. Hell, he had been fighting those thoughts for days. But was he mistaking her kiss for something more than what it was? Hell, what was it? He never should have given in to the urge to kiss her, but she had looked so damn desirable that he couldn't resist. Even now, if he closed her eyes, he could still see the serene smile on her face, hear the soft hum of her voice, and feel the warmth of her body pressed against his. And if she wasn't married? Well, he wouldn't have spent the last hour in the hotel bar, that was for damn sure!

Married. Jason had never in his life pursued a married woman. Never. How was he supposed to stay on this trip with her if he was attracted to her? How were they supposed to go back to the way they worked together only earlier today with this kiss hanging between them? Hell, how was he supposed to even look at himself in the mirror knowing he'd done something so disgraceful? How could he face her? How could he face his father when they got back to the office?

Once up in his room, Jason ripped off his tie and jacket and stalked the interior. He couldn't afford to let Maggie leave. He knew he would if she asked, no matter how much he'd hate it. Although...he knew he'd beg and grovel and make every promise he possibly could to convince her to stay. The truth was, she was too important to what he hoped to accomplish business-wise on this trip. But if he was going to survive the next couple of weeks, he was going to have to put some strict parameters on them so that they weren't in any more of these situations.

Booting up his tablet, he pulled up their itinerary. They had three days scheduled in Boston and then four in New York. The Boston meetings were going to be lengthy, but were in large groups and in offices; no chance of slow dancing and drinking there. Once in New York, their schedule was a little more open, and with a weekend in the middle, they'd have a day or so with nothing to do.

That could pose a problem.

What if he told her to call her husband and Jason would fly him in for the weekend? Maybe seeing the two of them together would be just what he needed to put everything into perspective and remind him of why he needed to keep his distance. Plus, wouldn't she want to see him by now? He didn't hang out with a lot of married couples, but he imagined a week apart was a lot. Perhaps bringing her husband here would make things right and she'd see that he actually respected her and her marriage.

The plan was perfect. Sighing with relief, he stripped and got ready for bed. Tomorrow, when they were en route to Boston, he'd surprise her with his idea. Maybe Maggie was just missing her husband and that was why she'd kissed him.

Lying down, Jason turned out the light, staring at the darkened ceiling and thinking about Maggie's lips on his and the man who had the right to kiss them any time he wanted. His final thought as sleep claimed him was, *Lucky bastard.*

From the moment Jason stepped out of the hotel room and met Maggie in the hall, he knew things were a little off. They both seemed uncomfortable and the ride down in the elevator bordered on painful. But once they stepped out into the lobby and he began asking about their schedule, things fell back into place. And by the time they were in the car and on the way to the airport, he could almost say they were back to normal.

On the plane, he got a call from one of his clients and excused himself while Maggie got everything set up and they prepared for takeoff.

He'd never been so thankful for a call in his life.

They were airborne and Maggie was pulling up the files that she wanted to review with Jason when he finally spoke.

"Listen, I was thinking, we're scheduled for three days in Boston, but realistically, we can be done in two. That means we can hit Manhattan on Saturday morning and then we don't have any meetings until Monday. Why don't you call your husband and I'll fly him up for the weekend?" He was quite proud of himself for thinking of it, and was anticipating her gratitude and how she'd be thankful for his consideration. But the look of pure horror on Maggie's face had him second guessing himself.

"What?" she cried. "Why? Why would you do that? We have a schedule to keep and there's no time to just change things around like that. It would be incredibly rude to rush through the meetings you already have scheduled. But more importantly, it's unnecessary. We have a lot to accomplish, and you're not paying me to have a weekend getaway. I told you I am more than capable of being on this trip without needing to have time with my husband, and I resent that you think otherwise."

Wow, protest much?

Clearing his throat, Jason shifted in his seat. "I just thought since we've been working so hard that maybe you would appreciate having a bit of a break. Most people at least get the weekend off. I honestly thought you'd like the idea," he said hesitantly.

"Well, it's not necessary. I am being well-compensated for working long hours on this trip and there's no need for you to go out of your way to change anything. If you would like to use the free time to do... whatever, then please feel free. I don't need to be entertained. We have enough work to keep me busy."

"Maggie, you're taking this all wrong," he said, leaning forward in his seat. "I'm trying to do something nice here."

"You treated me to a spa treatment yesterday. You took

me to an amazing event at the Rock and Roll Hall of Fame last night. I actually got to stand next to John Lennon's guitar! I'm traveling around the country to places that I've never seen before while staying at luxurious hotels, and I'm getting paid for it!" Her words were a little more clipped than usual.

Jason held up a hand to calm her down.

"I realize I was out of line last night," she said before he could say anything else. "I've apologized and I thought we could move on. I don't need you giving me some kind of special treatment to remind me of it."

"That wasn't what I was doing."

But... it was, and he knew it.

He just didn't expect her to realize it too.

"Okay, okay, I get it. Geez, it was just a thought. I'm sorry I brought it up." He watched as Maggie slowly calmed down, and now his curiosity was piqued even more. From what he'd learned so far, this mystery husband never danced with her, never traveled with her, apparently never called her, and she didn't have any inclination to spend time with him.

Hmm... That could also explain last night's kiss.

Frustrated wife? Bored with her husband? Did she even love this guy? Was he a good man, or was he a jerk? Or worse, abusive in some way? Jason felt ill. It didn't sit right with him. Even if Maggie wasn't happily married, it didn't give him the right to hit on her or for her to use him as some kind of substitute.

Who was he kidding? She wasn't using him for anything. She nearly left skid marks trying to get away from him last night, and even now was sitting as far away from him on the private plane as humanly possible, just like she had in the limo on the way back to the hotel and in the car this morning.

It was wishful thinking on his part that she was the one interested in him and not the other way around.

With the determination he was known for, Jason decided that the only way to keep his sanity was to push all personal thoughts of Maggie from his mind and focus on the business at hand. He was feeling confident about the upcoming meetings. He had to get his head back in the game if he wanted to move Montgomery's into a tax bracket that they'd never even dreamed of.

And that meant he needed to put all his focus on the task at hand.

Business.

Not pleasure.

Glancing up at Maggie, he frowned. She was reading something and nibbling on her bottom lip and he had to bite back a groan.

This was going to be harder than he thought.

"I can't believe that went so well," Maggie was saying on Friday evening as they took a cab back to their hotel. "That had to be the shortest meeting in history."

"Well, it helped that Dennis Michaels had more pressing matters to attend to," Jason said as he texted his brother Mac with an update.

"He should never have kept that appointment with us! His wife was in labor!"

Jason laughed. "We corporate types never like to miss an appointment," he teased. "Besides, it's their first child and those are notoriously slow in arriving."

Maggie nodded in agreement. "Well, between this meeting being over way earlier than expected and everyone else being so agreeable and ready to sign on the dotted line, we are actually ahead of schedule." She leaned back in her seat and sighed. "I wish all of our meetings would go like the ones here in Boston. Any chance we can put in a request for that?"

"If only." Jason hit the send button on his phone.

It was true, after a bumpy start to their trip, particularly on the business end of things, all of their client meetings had been flawless. He had been prepared for more disappointment, but the universe must have decided to cut him a break.

That didn't mean they had been relaxing, though. If anything, he and Maggie had spent a lot of time after each appointment meticulously analyzing what they'd said and done differently from their earlier ones. After far too many notes and a little obsessive over-thinking on his part, Jason felt like he now had the perfect script moving forward for the rest of the presentations. It was like a giant weight had been lifted off his shoulders.

Plus, he and Maggie were back on even ground. He felt like that whole night had just been a one-off and they were both just swept up in their surroundings. Lines had gotten blurred, but apparently they were both seeing things clearly. He was the boss and she was the assistant, and their working relationship was solid once again.

Now they had a lot of time to kill and since she completely shut down his idea of flying her husband out for the weekend, it had him thinking about what they could do to pass the time. This was the longest trip he'd taken, business-wise, and he was growing weary of being in corporate mode 24/7.

"I don't know about you, but as much as I've enjoyed our time here, I'm eager to hit New York City and spend some time there," he broached carefully, doing his best to gage her reaction. "You up for a late night drive?"

Her eyes went wide and for a moment she didn't say anything. "What about our flight tomorrow? Or our hotel reservation?"

"I'm tired of flying. I'll get us a car and we can grab something to eat on the road. It's a four-hour drive and—"

"We won't get in until close to midnight, Jason!" she said incredulously, even though he could tell she found the idea appealing. "Why don't we wait to fly tomorrow? I know we were flying commercial for it, but it's already booked."

"Because the flight isn't until noon, and with all the security stuff and having to be there two hours early…"

"I could look for an earlier flight," she suggested.

But he was holding his ground. "Then we're having to get up at the crack of dawn and that's a total drag too. If we stick to the original itinerary, we'll miss half the day there. There's so much to see and the weekend is wide open. The weather is supposed to be beautiful, and I want to walk around and eat pizza and grab hot dogs from a street vendor, shop a little."

"You shop?" she asked, clearly amused at the thought.

"Yes, I do," he said simply. "And there is no place better to shop than New York."

"I don't know about that, but I will admit that I'm looking forward to the food." Again, she nibbled on her bottom lip like she tended to do when she was thinking hard about something. "And I've never really spent a lot of time in the city."

"There's a lot to see, Maggie," he encouraged. "We

could casually stroll around or we can play tourists and try to see all the sites you want. Maybe see a show?" Honestly, he had no idea if that was something that even interested her, but he was hoping to hit on something to make her say yes.

"I've never seen a Broadway show," she said thoughtfully. "But I'm not really a musical kind of girl."

"O-kay..."

She looked up at him. "And you're sure you want to do this? It's been a busy couple of weeks and you haven't had any down time either. Are you sure you're up to a four hour drive?"

"Is that a yes? Ready for a road trip?" he asked excitedly, forgetting about his earlier intentions of keeping his distance.

"Oh, what the hell!" she said with equal abandon. "It beats watching another night of bad cable."

"Atta girl."

Jason knew how to make things happen. Within the hour, there was a rental car waiting for them at their hotel and an hour after that, they were packed and ready to go. Maggie had made arrangements to get sandwiches for the trip from the hotel restaurant, and by seven o'clock, they were on the road.

Jason had been on the phone most of the time they were getting ready, and Maggie had to wonder who he was talking to. By the time they were hitting the I-90, she had their food and drinks situated so Jason could eat and drive. They talked amicably about some of the sites they hoped to see, and while she was secretly thrilled to have the free time to explore New York City, she knew she couldn't let herself get too carried away. She was on company time, no matter what Jason said.

Jason.

How wise was it for her to be actively making plans to spend time with him outside of work? Granted, it was the weekend, and they were traveling together, but she sort of expected them to get to the city and for him to go his way and for her to go hers. In her wildest dreams, she never imagined him actually looking to spend more time with her.

Especially after her transgression.

Ugh... just thinking about how she'd thrown herself at him still made her cringe, but fortunately Jason hadn't mentioned it again and it was clear he was willing to forget about it.

If only I could...

Hell, she thought about it all the time. Every night when she was in bed, every morning before she left her room to meet him, and sometimes when they were in a meeting and he was in the middle of a presentation, she could swear she could still feel his lips on hers.

Inwardly, she groaned. *I seriously have a problem...*

And as much as she knew it was safer for them to stay in work mode, their conversation once they were on the road dealt more with favorite places and landmarks located in New York City and ones they'd been to already versus ones they hoped to see. Music played softly in the background as they talked about concerts they'd seen and who was on their bucket list.

Then the conversation turned to sports.

"Well, you already know I'm a New York Rangers fan," Maggie said as she popped the last bite of her chocolate chip cookie into her mouth. "Any chance I get to see them play, I try to make it. Other than that, though, I'm not really into sports."

"I can sit and watch almost any sport and typically decide on the spot who I'm rooting for," he explained. "I played football and baseball in high school and college, but it was never with the dream of going into the major or national leagues."

"What was it like when Lucas played?"

"I thought he was crazy. It just wasn't a lifestyle I'm comfortable with, but my brother lived for it. That was why it was so devastating for him when he got injured and couldn't play again. It took him a lot of years to get over that psychologically."

"I'm sure," Maggie agreed. "It was his whole life."

He nodded. "Yeah, but now he and Emma are married and... she's been really good for him. I mean, it's great to have a career you're passionate about, but it shouldn't be your entire life."

"Says the workaholic," she teased.

Fortunately, he didn't take offense and the conversation moved on to other places in the US she'd like to visit. The conversation flowed and it just made Jason seem that much more attractive. She'd never dated a man who she could just sit and talk to like this. None of it was awkward, and none of it felt forced. They were just two people who enjoyed conversing on many different topics.

By the time she saw the lights of the city, she was sleepy and yet too excited to close her eyes. There was so much to see and do, and she felt the energy of the city consuming her already. Soon they were deep in the heart of the city, and she nearly choked when she saw where they were.

"The Four Seasons? We're staying at the *Four Seasons*?" she squealed. "That wasn't on our itinerary, Jason!"

He laughed as he climbed from the car and smiled at the valet, who was helping Maggie out. "Well, our hotel couldn't accommodate us for tonight, so I made some calls and got us in here. You're not disappointed, are you?"

Maggie burst out laughing and nearly fell over. "Yes, Jason, I am extremely disappointed that I have to stay at one of the top luxury hotels in the world. Damn you." She barely got the sentence out before breaking out in a fit of giggles again.

Jason walked around the car and grabbed her hand, something that felt far too natural, and led her into the lobby. "Now behave yourself," he teased as he walked to the desk to check them in.

She wanted to look at everything and practically tripped over her own two feet because she was looking up rather than where they were going. No doubt she looked like a typical tourist walking across the lobby, but she didn't care. When they stopped at the front desk, she leaned against it before turning around and taking it all in again.

"Welcome to the Four Seasons, Mr. Montgomery. We have two rooms waiting for you for five nights—"

"Five nights?" Maggie interrupted, instantly turning back to face him. "You completely canceled the other reservation?"

Jason nodded and then shrugged. "This is where I really wanted to stay anyway," he said simply.

"Then why didn't you book it in the first place?"

Another shrug. "It seemed impractical at the time, but now that we've been on the road for a while, I thought we deserved an upgrade."

It made sense, but suddenly Maggie felt like a country bumpkin. She was dressed casually, and even in her best clothes she had brought with her, she felt hyperaware of the fact that she was completely out of her element here.

Jason saw the apprehension on her face and questioned it.

"I wasn't mentally prepared for this, Jason," she said quietly, the thrill of being surrounded by so much luxury gone. "I don't belong here."

"Nonsense," was all he said as he accepted their room keys and followed the bellboy to the elevators. "And tomorrow, let's just sleep in and start the day whenever we're ready."

She instantly agreed. It was late and they were both exhausted. She was at a loss for words on the ride up in the elevator, and as they said their goodbyes by their doors, Maggie told herself to simply relax and enjoy this because she'd most likely never have the opportunity to stay in a hotel like this ever again.

In his own room, Jason tipped the bellhop and thanked him before quietly closing the door behind him. Leaning against it, he took in the room and let out a long sigh.

Maybe he'd gone a little overboard by booking The Four Seasons. There were hundreds of hotels in Manhattan and he could have chosen any one of them that were on par with the ones they'd been staying at so far on this trip. But a part of him had wanted to do this, and not just because it was one of his favorite places to stay in the city.

He wanted to impress Maggie.

"Shit," he murmured, raking a hand through his hair.

Pushing away from the door, he slowly walked around the room and decided unpacking could wait until the morning. It was late and he was tired and maybe a good night's sleep would put things into perspective.

"Right. Because that's worked so well for me already," he mumbled as he kicked his shoes off.

It didn't matter if he slept for four hours or fourteen, he had a feeling it wouldn't be enough. He had a lot to accomplish this weekend, hopefully relaxing and maybe figuring out what was behind his assistant's apprehensiveness whenever the subject of her husband came up. Even though he had promised himself he'd stay focused strictly on business, he wouldn't be satisfied until he knew the truth about the woman who was consuming all of his thoughts.

FIVE

ONCE AGAIN, they had adjoining rooms, but had agreed to sleep in on Saturday morning since they had arrived late the previous evening. Maggie was completely on board with that plan because she was totally exhausted and the bed in her room was the most comfortable one she had ever slept on.

As much as she had planned on sleeping late, she woke up at a conservative nine o'clock and ordered herself some breakfast. The thought of calling Jason and seeing if he was awake crossed her mind, but she was kind of enjoying the little bit of space and freedom she had.

"A little distance is a good thing," she told herself. Maybe if she didn't call him at all, he'd go out on his own and she could have the entire day to do her own thing and not spend it being so hyper-aware of him.

The snort was out before she could stop it.

Even on the other side of the door, she was hyper-aware of him

They were back on track professionally. She knew that. The kiss was seemingly forgotten. Out of sight, out of mind, she supposed. But at night? It was the highlight of all of her dreams. Sure, during the day Maggie was able to play the part of the engrossed executive assistant, but once she was alone with her thoughts? They were filled with one Jason Montgomery.

When he had taken her hand last night and led her into the hotel? There was a moment where she wished they were there as a couple instead of colleagues. That he was leading her up to a room where they would spend the night making love instead of making plans to meet up for hot dogs on Fifth Avenue.

Groaning, she told herself to stop with the romantic fantasies. It would never happen, and she needed to get a grip. She needed to finish this trip and honor her commitment, but there was a very real possibility that she would need to either talk to his father when she got back about moving to another position, or simply leaving Montgomery's all together. Because no matter how hard she tried, when she closed her eyes, she could feel his lips on hers, the way his strong arms had embraced her, the smell of his cologne.

Dammit.

"Okay, enough of that," she chastised herself as she finished her cup of fresh fruit. Once she was done eating, she gathered her toiletries and decided to truly get her day started.

Taking the time to shower in the magnificent spa quality bathroom, Maggie felt that she would be just fine spending the day in there! The knowledge that she had five days to luxuriate in this kind of atmosphere was making her giddy.

By eleven she was dressed, ready, and more than a little eager to go outside and explore the Big Apple. She called Jason's room and was surprised when he told her he'd been up since seven waiting for her call. They agreed to meet down in the lobby and she told him she was more than willing to let him play tour guide.

And hoped that involved him holding her hand the entire time.

Bad Maggie!

Dressed in jeans and sneakers, she was ready to walk for however long Jason planned. "Was there any place in particular that you absolutely want to see?" he asked as he put on a pair of sunglasses and walked out the front door of the hotel.

"Everything!" Maggie said with a bright smile. "I'm just excited to have a day to do this!"

"Remember that you said that," he said with a wicked grin, took a moment to get his bearings, and then took her hand and led her out onto the streets of New York.

She had to bite back the smile as his hand curled around hers.

Four hours later, she was ready to drop. She collapsed on a sidewalk café bistro table and just tried to catch her breath. "Okay, I know I said that I wanted to see everything, but I didn't really mean it." She paused. "Go. Save yourself. I'll grab a cab once I can breathe again."

Jason sat down opposite her and ordered them each a sparkling water. "Don't quit on me now. We've barely scratched the surface!"

"Scratched the surface? Jason, I am dazzled by all that we've seen, but surely, we can catch a cab for some of it."

"It's not the same," he said sweetly.

And while she knew he was right, she'd be willing to make the sacrifice for the sake of having the ability to walk.

"What I planned next for us..."

"We've seen Times Square, we've walked in Central

Park, we've eaten pizza and hot dogs." She stopped to breathe. "Then there was Rockefeller Center and Radio City Music Hall. I think I am done for the day. I may need to go and soak my feet in my tub-slash-swimming pool."

"Well, you could do that, but if you do, you're going to miss out on the best part," he teased.

She glared at him. "Best part? You mean we haven't seen the best part yet? What are you holding out on me?"

"Well, I was able to make some calls this morning and I got us two tickets to the Rangers' game tonight!"

Her heart kicked hard in her chest and she knew her eyes were bugging out. "No way!" she said excitedly. "Seriously? You're not joking with me?"

"I would never joke about tickets to a sporting event. It wouldn't be right."

"Damn straight it wouldn't. *Oh, my gosh*! We're going to Madison Square Garden! I'm going to see the Rangers play on home ice!" She then began to ramble eagerly, asking Jason a dozen questions in a row about the rest of their day.

"Slow down there, slugger," he joked. "We'll head back to the hotel so you can rest for a little while and then we can grab dinner someplace and then..."

"Dinner someplace? Dinner someplace? Are you crazy?" Maggie looked at him as if he'd lost his mind. "We are going to have the full game experience, and that includes eating from the concession stands in the Garden."

He wanted to laugh and tease her some more about the whole thing, but honestly, he found her reaction to such a simple thing as a hockey game refreshing. Some women would fish for a nice dinner out before the game or want to avoid the game altogether, and yet here was Maggie, completely over the moon because they were going to eat hot dogs at Madison Square Garden so she could cheer on her team.

Yet another reason he was finding it hard to not be drawn to her.

"I cannot believe that you got us tickets," she said as she sipped her water. "This is the best day ever!" Taking a quick swallow, Maggie placed the glass down and looked at Jason. "Thank you. In case I forget to thank you later, I just want you to know right now how much this means to me."

If her words didn't say it, her eyes certainly conveyed it. "You are more than welcome, Maggie. I have to admit, I've never been to a game at the Garden, so you'll have to play tour guide this evening."

"Deal," she agreed readily. "Now, let's agree to take a cab back to the hotel so we can rest up for later."

Jason stood and then playfully pulled Maggie to her feet. "Deal."

The transformation was remarkable, and Jason found that in a crowd of eighteen thousand screaming hockey fans, he was speechless.

Somehow between the time he had dropped Maggie off at her room and the time they met to leave for the game, she had gone from mild-mannered assistant to rabid hockey fan! Her hair was loose and she wore a New York Rangers sweatshirt with jeans and sneakers, and if he listened closely enough, he could almost swear that she had suddenly picked up a New York accent.

"Off sides! *Off sides!*" she yelled at the top of her lungs as she jumped to her feet and Jason sat back and smiled. "Dammit," she muttered as the play was stopped and the crowd settled a bit. Without taking her eyes from the ice, Maggie reached for her beer and then sat down on the edge of her seat.

While Jason had the urge to say something, anything, that would allow him to interact with her, for all intents and purposes, she didn't even realize he was there.

Talk about an ego buster.

"For the love of it, stop playing with the puck!" she called out, and Jason simply sat and watched in fascination. "Icing? Seriously? Come on!"

He'd say she was overzealous, but pretty much everyone around them was yelling out the same things.

He was the only one who was quiet, but that was because Montgomerys didn't jump up and yell or hurl insults during sporting events. Sure, they had cheered wildly for Lucas when he played in the NFL, but that was for his brother. This team of hockey players meant nothing to him, so...he didn't see the point of getting overly involved. They were playing and knew what they were doing. Nothing he had to say was going to change the game for them.

Clearly. he was in the minority at Madison Square Garden because everyone had something to say. And as Maggie hurled one last expletive down at the ice when the period ended, he knew he'd never forget it.

In between periods, they trolled the Garden to purchase more snacks and beer and Maggie was content to take it all in. When she did talk to Jason, it was about the game, the players, the building itself and although it wasn't a topic that he felt overly informed about, he was happy to watch Maggie enjoying herself.

By the third period, he could tell her voice was raw from all the yelling. Half of her phrases were unintelligible and he knew she'd be feeling the effects of this night well into tomorrow. But she continued to drink her beer and eat nachos and yell even without a voice. He tried to tell himself it was like going to a game with his buddies. He'd gone to football games, baseball games, and an occasional basketball game. All his friends were sports enthusiasts, so Maggie's behavior was nothing new to him.

She's a friend.

I'm at a game with a friend.

He knew he was lying because he'd never once checked out his friends' asses or leaned in because they smelled so good.

Still, it was all good and he simply enjoyed knowing he did something nice for a friend.

A colleague.

A business associate.

But when the final buzzer rang out and she turned and jumped into his arms in celebration, Jason knew he was lying to himself.

And that he was in serious trouble.

It had been a perfect night for Rangers fans, with a 4–1 victory over Philadelphia. As the final buzzer sounded out, Maggie jumped up along with the thousands of other fans to cheer and then jumped into Jason's arms. He caught her easily and found her excitement and enthusiasm to be contagious. "We won!" she cried hoarsely. When she realized what she had done, she disentangled herself from Jason and joined the throngs of people walking from their seats. Maggie was simply glowing with victory as they exited their row. "That was amazing," she gushed. "Wasn't that a great game, Jace?"

He agreed. "I have to admit, there is definitely a vibe here in the Garden I can't imagine feeling anyplace else. New York fans are something else."

"You know it. They're the best!" Making their way through the mass exodus was time-consuming, and finally Maggie just stopped and dropped into a vacant seat. Jason stood for a moment in confusion.

"Are you okay?"

She looked up at him. "What? Oh, yeah, I'm fine. It's going to take a while for the crowd to thin out, so I figured what's the rush?" She sighed and looked around the grand arena. "Think of the history of this place," she said in a near whisper. "How many games, events, and concerts has it seen? The number of people who've been here... it's amazing."

Jason sat down in the row in front of her and looked around. He'd never even given a thought to where he watched his sports, but the look of wonder on Maggie's face had him contemplating her words.

"I know it sounds silly and a bit clichéd, but it would be amazing if these walls could talk," she said softly, more to herself than to Jason. They sat for several minutes in companionable silence that they both seemed to need. With a quiet sigh, Maggie stood and stretched. "Ready to fight the crowds once again?"

Jason stood and nodded. "I think we'll be okay; it's pretty empty in here already." Wordlessly, they walked up the steps to the nearest exit and he noticed how Maggie took one more wistful look over her shoulder before walking through the doors. He wished there was something he could say, something insightful, but decided just to let her have her moment.

They were outside finally and Maggie was a bit chilled, but the thought of finding a cab seemed daunting. Jason read the indecision on her face. "It's not as hard as it seems. The trick is to walk a couple of blocks away from all the crowds and then hail one."

She nodded. "That makes sense." They walked silently up Seventh Avenue toward Times Square. The city was so alive, there was something so magical about it at night. How had she lived so long without experiencing so much? The way she lived had never really bothered her before, but now? Traveling with Jason? She realized there was an entire world out there that she was missing out on because of her self-imposed exile.

Before she knew it, Jason had stopped and a cab was pulling up beside them. She climbed in and listened as he told the driver where to take them and then sat back, watching the city streets speed by. She didn't realize that she'd let out a sigh until Jason spoke.

"Did you want to walk some more?"

"Oh, no, it's just that there's so much to see. My feet are sore and I know taking a cab is the right choice..."

"But..." he prompted.

She smiled, "But I like to think that I'm superhuman and could handle walking the mile and a half back to the hotel."

Jason chuckled. "Well, if we hadn't walked so much today, I might have considered it, but I'm not as super-human as I'd like to be either. I think tomorrow my body is going to be cursing me."

Maggie laughed out loud and Jason joined her. When they arrived back at the hotel, they commiserated like an elderly couple about all of their aches and pains, and Maggie was having a fit of the giggles by the time the elevator stopped at their floor.

Outside of her door, she took a deep breath and turned to face Jason. "Thank you so much for such an incredible night. It was absolutely the best. This was a bucket list thing for me."

He arched a dark brow at her. "Seriously? It was hot dogs and fistfights!"

"Are you crazy?" she laughed. "It was a chance to do something that I've always wanted to do! It wasn't about the food, per se, it was about the entire experience. I finally got to experience a night at the Garden as an adult who got to scream and yell and watch her team win!" Maggie caught herself before she flung herself at Jason and hugged him again. She enjoyed doing that too much.

With a steadying breath, she opened her door. "Anyway, it was a fabulous night, Jason. Thank you for making the time for us to do this. I'm sure there were other things you would have preferred to do, but I appreciate you making the time to do this for me." Her tone was serious, as was the expression in her eyes. She stood there staring at him for a long moment and almost caved and leaned toward him, something that he seemed about to do himself. The air seemed warmer, the tension thicker, and if she wasn't mistaken, this was exactly like what had happened at the gala. Did she really want to tempt fate twice?

Yes.

No!

Regretfully, she took a step back. "Good night," she whispered and went into her room and closed the door, hating herself the entire time.

❧

Jason stood in the hallway staring at Maggie's door for far longer than he should have. He was confused and disappointed and didn't know why. It was the sound of voices coming off of the elevator that finally had him moving to his own room, and once inside he was too keyed up to go to sleep.

Glancing at the bedside clock, he noticed that it was barely eleven. It was late, but not too late to call the one person who could shed a little light on who exactly Maggie Barrett was.

Kicking off his shoes, Jason pulled out his cell phone and scrolled through his contacts until he found who he wanted, then relaxed on the bed and waited.

"Jason?" his father said by way of greeting. "Is everything okay? It's a little late for a social call."

"Hey, Dad," he said easily, the sound of his father's voice bringing a smile to his face. "I'm fine. I just wanted to check in and see how you were doing."

"At eleven at night? Lucky for you I'm in the study and your mother is upstairs reading, otherwise she'd think there was some sort of terrible emergency that had you calling so late at night."

"Stop with the theatrics, Dad," Jason chided softly. "I know it's a bit late but…"

"Are you sure everything's okay? Is it the meetings? Are they going all right? I haven't seen any red flags in what you've been sending in."

"No, no…it's not the meetings; everything is fine there."

William was silent for a moment. "So, where are you now? Still in Boston? You're due in New York on Monday, right?"

"Actually, we're in New York now. We drove down late last night after our last meeting and decided to relax this weekend." Jason couldn't hide the smile in his voice. "I took Maggie to a hockey game tonight."

"Hockey?" William said in disbelief. "Why on earth would you take Maggie to a hockey game?"

Jason laughed. "Believe it or not, she's a fan. For a woman who is quiet and unassuming during the day, she is a rabid hockey fan when she's watching her team play. It was quite an eye-opening experience."

Something in his son's tone caught William's attention. "So, she's a hockey fan, huh? Who would've guessed? I can't imagine her sitting there in one of her conservative outfits, hair all pulled back, yelling and cheering for her team."

"There was no conservative outfit, Dad. She wore her hair all loose and wavy and a pair of jeans and a New York Rangers sweatshirt... She fit right in. She was like a kid in a candy shop. We ate hot dogs and pretzels and drank beer and Maggie said it was the best night." Jason sighed. "I never met a woman who was content just to eat hot dogs and drink beer."

William was glad Jason could not see him grinning like the cat that had eaten the canary. "Not all women want to be wined and dined, Jace. Maggie's a sensible girl with simple tastes. I'm sure she's unimpressed with the whole concept of spending a lot of money frivolously."

His father's words made sense, but Jason had a ton of questions that he needed answered if he was going to figure Maggie out. "No, you're right; Maggie's definitely not impressed with money. We're at the Four Seasons and she just about freaked out on me for spending the money."

William chuckled. "Sounds just like her. How did you end up there? That wasn't on your itinerary."

Jason explained about how their last-minute change of plans had dictated the change in hotels. "The thing is, I never gave much thought to where we stayed. All our lives we've stayed at some of the finest hotels in the world and to me, they're just a place to sleep, but the look of awe and wonder on Maggie's face when we walked in? It was price-less." An image of that face came to Jason's mind. "Then she was embarrassed because she didn't think she was good enough to stay here."

"Well, I hope you convinced her otherwise!" his father scolded.

"Of course I did! Geez, what do you take me for? An idiot?" Jason sat up and raked a hand through his hair. "Look, there are some things about Maggie that just don't... fit."

William waited.

And waited.

"Like what?" he finally asked.

"Okay, for starters, there's the fact that she's even on this trip with me."

"I don't understand. Why is that a problem?"

"It goes back to that initial interview. Why has she worked for us for so long and I'm just now seeing and hearing about her? How could you leave her down in customer service for so long when she is clearly such an asset to the company?"

"It wasn't my decision to make, Jason. Maggie didn't want to be an assistant; she was happy working in a low-pressure job. It was what she wanted."

"But why? She's so talented and intelligent! What happened at her last job to make her want to hide away in a mindless position?"

"That's not for me to discuss with you."

"Seriously, Dad? You're not going to give me anything?"

"Like I said, it's not my place. Son or not, it's a matter of privacy. Have you asked her?"

"What? No!" Jason nearly shouted, frustrated that his father wasn't giving him any information at all. "Look, you seem to know Maggie much better than I do, and I'm asking you to help me fill in some blanks!"

"Jason, she's your assistant. You work with her every day. Surely you must have some down time where you're not talking about business."

"I'm telling you, we spent the entire day together and we talked non-stop, but I don't know, on some levels I feel like I know so much about her and in other ways, I still don't know a damn thing."

"Why don't you ask about her personal life or whatever it is specifically that you'd like to know?" He paused before murmuring, "Although for the life of me, I have no idea why you're so curious..."

"Because when I do ask anything personal, she changes. I can't quite explain it, but any mention of her personal life and she just sort of goes blank, like she's really uncomfortable talking about it. I even tried inviting her husband up here for the weekend and she nearly bit my head off!"

William stifled a laugh. "I think maybe you're over-exaggerating, Jason. Why would she be mad about you inviting her husband to come to New York for the weekend?"

"That's what I'd like to know! If you ask me, this guy must be a world-class jackass."

"Now this I have to hear. Why, exactly?"

Where did he even begin? Jason stood and began pacing the large room. "Okay, first, he let her come on this trip."

"And that makes him a jackass?" William asked with

amusement. "If you remember correctly, you specifically asked for a married assistant who would travel with you. We found you one! How could that be a bad thing?"

"It's not that it's bad, not really, but he just doesn't seem to care that she's away. From what I can tell, he doesn't call her and she doesn't call him. Doesn't that seem odd to you? You call Mom every day!"

"Well, your mother and I aren't like a lot of married couples. Maggie's young. I'm assuming her husband is young as well. How do you know they aren't calling one another?"

"Because I never see her on the phone!"

"Are you sharing a room with her?" William asked innocently.

"Dammit, Dad, you know I'm not. Why would you even say such a thing?"

"I'm just saying, Jace, that you have no idea what she's doing in her room when she's away from you. For all you know, she's curled up in bed right now, all relaxed and sweet talking her husband."

That image lodged itself in Jason's mind and made him angry. His hands were clenched at his sides and he wanted to walk to the door connecting their rooms, kick down Maggie's door, and see if that was the case. His father's voice was the only thing stopping him.

"You can't get angry at Maggie for doing what you asked," William sweetly reminded his son.

"What the hell did I ask?"

"You made it clear that you didn't want to waste time dealing with a needy spouse. Sounds to me like she is following your rules, not spending her work hours on the phone and keeping her personal life separate from your business hours."

When his father said it, it made sense, but to Jason it still didn't seem to fit. "Okay, sure, fine, I guess that could be how it is," he said finally.

"But…" William prompted.

"We went to a benefit the other night," Jason began, "and we danced." For a brief moment, Jason swore he could still feel Maggie in his arms, and then remembered that he was supposed to be proving a point to his father. "And she said the last time she danced was in high school at her prom."

"O-kay…"

"High school, Dad! That was like… what… ten years ago? How is that possible?"

William let out a hearty laugh. "Son, I'm sure you're trying to tell me something, but for the life of me, I don't know what it is!"

"Married couples dance! At their wedding, on dates, or whatever," he said defensively. "How is it that Maggie could be married and not have danced since high school?"

"Maybe her husband's a poor dancer?"

"Or maybe he's just a jerk," Jason countered. "Look, all I'm saying is that the guy seems to show absolutely no interest in Maggie. Any time we go anywhere or do anything, it's like she's… living for the first time! I have to be honest with you, Dad, I'm worried about her."

"Well, Jason, to be honest right back at you, it's *you* I'm worried about."

"Me? Why?"

William let out a dramatic sigh. "You asked for an assistant who would not come on to you. We found you one. You asked for an assistant who is married. We found you one. You basically wanted a completely uncomplicated business companion who had no interest in you personally and yet here you are, attacking Maggie's personal life. She's your assistant; she's nothing to you. Leave her personal life alone, it's none of your concern." His tone was mild, but his words were meant to provoke.

"What the hell is the matter with you?" Jason snapped. "Maggie's more than just an assistant to me! She's..."

And then he caught himself and wished that he could take his words back.

Dammit.

"Jason," William said, suddenly serious. "Maggie *is* just your assistant, right? You haven't done anything to change that, have you?"

His father knew him too well, and Jason knew that lying would be pointless. "It wasn't supposed to be like this," he admitted quietly. "I liked her work ethic, I enjoyed our conversations, and then we started this trip and suddenly I'm getting to know her and I feel... connected to her somehow. I look forward to spending time with her and getting to know her, and then I have to remind myself she's married and I realize I'm no better than all of those women who've worked for me these last months."

"You are nothing like that, Jace," his father replied solemnly. "I don't want you to put yourself down." He paused. "How does Maggie feel?"

Once again, Jason knew it would be pointless to lie. "I think she maybe feels the same way but... she's married, Dad. I would never, ever do anything to jeopardize her marriage."

William took a deep breath and slowly let it out. "Talk to Maggie," he said simply.

"But..."

"Talk to her."

"To what end, Dad? She's married; she's my assistant. There is no way this can end well."

William repeated his words. "Trust me. The two of you need to have an open and honest conversation. All relationships—even work ones—require trust. You need to do this."

If only it were that easy. "It's getting late," he finally said, suddenly feeling mentally and physically exhausted.

"Think about what I said, Jace."

"I will, Dad. Thanks for talking to me. Send Mom my love."

"I will. Good night."

Jason powered down his phone, stripped, and climbed into the king-sized bed. Flipping the lights off, he rested against the pillows and stared into the darkness, wondering just what he was going to do about this situation.

His father said he should talk to her, but he honestly had no idea what he'd even say. And if he did it now while they were on this trip with more time left on it, there was a good chance it would make things ridiculously awkward.

Sighing loudly, he whispered, "What do I do?"

He was a man used to being in control, a man who knew how to overcome every obstacle thrown in his path. Unfortunately, this was not a simple case of overcoming some red tape in a business deal or appeasing a difficult client.

This was about his heart.

This was about Maggie's marriage.

This was about a situation that would leave somebody hurt. And Jason didn't want to be responsible for that.

He had to force himself to put his focus back on his business.

Again.

To remember that Maggie was off-limits, no matter how much she tempted him.

Again.

But most important, Jason had to remember that for the first time possibly in his life, he wasn't going to get what he wanted.

SIX

FIVE MORE DAYS.

Jason stared out his hotel window overlooking the Atlanta skyline and let out a weary sigh. Those first few days immediately following the hockey game had been the hardest of his life. While being a hardass had never been a problem for him before, it was suddenly one now when the one he was being hard on stared back at him with sadness and confusion written in her big brown eyes.

It had taken every ounce of strength he possessed not to cave in.

Not that he had been mean, no; Jason had gone into extreme workaholic mode and spent every waking moment doing nothing that wasn't directly related to Montgomerys and the expansion project. They could probably go home right now and skip these last few days of meetings. Things had gone so well as they'd traveled down the East Coast that Jason didn't feel they'd be missing out on anything. He had more than enough business to make him happy.

But no, being the ultimate planner and perfectionist, and knowing that he always finished what he started, Jason knew he had to get through these last five days, even if it killed him.

And it just might.

To her credit, Maggie never outright questioned Jason about his abrupt change in behavior. When they'd met for breakfast that Sunday morning in New York, he'd made sure that he was deeply entrenched in his agenda for their upcoming meetings. He'd questioned her lack of prepared-ness and had actually sent her back to her room to get her laptop so that she could get some work done after their day off.

For the nine days that had followed, Jason had worked like a man possessed. He was up before dawn on most days and would utilize the hotel gym before starting work. By the time he met up with Maggie daily, he had already gone through an hour of the only physical release he could manage. He pushed his body to its limits every morning and then did the same to his brain throughout the day until he fell into an exhausted sleep every night.

And still it wasn't enough to take the edge off of what he was feeling for her.

Jason was careful to keep them from participating in any social settings as they had early in their trip. Although he had a couple of charitable events on their agenda, he'd managed to exclude Maggie from them under the guise of needing her to prepare contracts and reports that were vital to their project.

Well, he laughed at himself mirthlessly, they weren't vital to the project quite as much as they were vital to helping him keep his distance. And his sanity. Maggie never argued and actually seemed relieved not to have to traipse along with him everywhere he went. While Jason knew deep down that he should have taken his father's advice and actually talked to her, he just couldn't bring himself to do it.

Five more days.

It might as well be a damn lifetime.

Turning from his view from the top floor of the Loews Atlanta, Jason looked around the room. It was beautiful; it was luxurious. It was far too big for a man alone. The king-size bed only emphasized that he was sleeping alone and he didn't like it. If he really wanted to, there was no doubt Jason could go out and find company for the evening.

But he didn't want company, he wanted Maggie.

Dammit.

The bedside clock showed it was nearing midnight, and Jason was too keyed up to sleep. He couldn't wait to get back to Charlotte: back to his own home and his own bed and his own life. Maybe once he was back in his own surroundings, this obsession would end. Maybe once they were back to working in the office and not spending so much time with only one another for company, Jason would be free to pick up the phone and call a woman for a date without wishing she were someone else.

Maybe he would lose his mind before they ever got home.

Five more days.

Maggie was miserable.

Looking down at her calendar app, she saw there were only five days left on the trip and hoped she'd survive them.

While Jason was doing exactly what he was supposed to be doing, being her boss, she missed the camaraderie that they had shared early in the trip. She kicked herself daily for letting her guard down and allowing herself to have feelings for him.

In her own defense, Jason Montgomery was an incredible man. He was kind and funny and intelligent, the type of man who really took an interest in you when he wanted to. And for a couple of days there, he seemed to really want to know Maggie.

Then he didn't.

She was certain it was her own fault. After all, here she was, a supposedly married woman who couldn't seem to stop throwing herself at him. She was the exact thing Jason had been trying to avoid on this trip. It was no wonder he barely looked at her. He was probably trying to think of ways to send her home and possibly move her back to the customer service department.

That thought was more than a little depressing, and she let out a sigh. It was late and she was sitting alone in her hotel room, curled up in a chair. Not that long ago, if anyone had told her she'd be staying in a luxury hotel and working as an executive assistant for an attractive man, she would have snorted with disbelief. Add the fact that she was the one attracted to the boss and not the other way around, and she would have laughed out loud. And yet, here she was.

They had less than a week left on the trip. Three days in Atlanta, two in Miami, and then it was back home. What would happen then? She couldn't imagine Jason would fire her immediately. No, they still had a lot of work to do on this expansion project once they were back at Montgomery's. But once the project was wrapped up and it was back to business as usual, then what? Could she go to his father and request a transfer back to her old position? Would Jason beat her to the punch and do it for her?

And sadly, she sort of wished he'd decide for her.

Standing, she walked over to her mini fridge, pulled out a bottle of water, and took a long drink. She didn't want to go back to her old life, not really. The woman she had been before this trip was a scared woman, a shell of a person. She wasn't living. She'd had no friends. These last weeks with Jason opened her eyes to how much there was to do and see, and she was missing it all because of the actions of one person. But now, she was done letting that bastard have any control over her life.

Placing the water on her nightstand, she went about getting ready for bed. Walking into the bathroom, she turned on the light and then took a long, hard look at her reflection. She was too young to hide away from life any longer. While she didn't have a clue what to do about Jason and her feelings for him, she knew that when they got back home, she was going to start getting involved in things. She'd finally accept some of those after work invitations her co-workers were always extending. Maybe she'd join a gym, take a class or two, and start going out more.

Reaching for her toothbrush, she couldn't shake the image of the person she wanted to go out with the most.

Jason.

"You have to let that go," she scolded her reflection. "He's your boss and that's all he is ever going to be. He thinks you're married, for crying out loud. How are you going to explain that one?"

She'd really backed herself into a corner. At the time it had made perfect sense, but now that she was ready for a change, Maggie realized how that one little lie was going to complicate her life in a major way.

At least where Jason was concerned.

For now, she had no choice but to continue with the

ruse. It had kept her from doing something completely foolish with Jason, and as much as she hated to admit it, it was probably for the best that they hadn't fallen into bed together on this trip. It would only make things more difficult and confusing when they got home.

Unfortunately, the image of him in bed had her heart racing. Maybe it would have been worth the difficulty and confusion, even if it had turned out only to be for one night.

She slipped into her pajamas and turned out the lights as she climbed into bed. It was ridiculously large for one person and although it was a complete luxury, Maggie had a feeling it would even be more decadent to share it with someone.

Naked.

Rolling onto her side, she couldn't help but punch her pillow out of frustration before settling in for yet another night filled with dreams of the one man she wanted but couldn't have.

Five more days.

SEVEN

THEY'D MADE it through the Atlanta meeting and were landing in Miami. Jason spent most of the flight on the phone with his brother Mac while Maggie typed up last-minute contracts at Jason's request.

They checked into their hotel and rushed up to their rooms without exchanging a word. Maggie had just enough time to freshen up her makeup before Jason knocked on the door to signal that the car was waiting. She sighed with irritation. Did he really think one word from him would have her throwing herself at him? Couldn't he at least have the common decency to say something to her that wasn't directly about Montgomerys? It was getting beyond rude and Maggie wasn't sure if she'd be able to make it through another day like this.

When she stepped out of her room, Jason was already halfway down the hall. She practically had to run to catch up with him at the elevator, and when they stepped on and he hung up the phone, she stamped her hand over the emergency stop button and faced Jason full of fury.

"What the hell, Maggie?" he snapped. "What are you doing?"

"You know, Jason, I think I deserve a little more common courtesy than a knock on the door beckoning me to follow you."

Jason pinched the bridge of his nose and inhaled sharply. "We don't have time for this right now. We have an appointment to get to."

"Oh, I get that; believe me, I do. What I don't get is why I'm being treated like some sort of leper or something! I've been working my butt off for you on this trip and in the last week you have been impossible and just flat out rude!"

His eyes finally met hers. "Rude? Look, I don't know what you were expecting on this trip, but I've been treating you like an employee. We are on this trip to work. I'll admit that I got a little sidetracked back in New York, but then I realized it was a mistake. I hired you to be my assistant; not my date, not my friend. You are an employee of Montgomery's and you were chosen for this position because you met certain criteria."

"Because I'm *married*?" she said snidely, wanting nothing more than to smack his face and make him stop using that condescending tone on her.

"That was partially it. You were qualified for the job that I needed done. I told you from the get-go this wasn't a pleasure trip and I think for a while there the lines were getting blurred." It was the most honest statement he'd ever made to her, and the look of horror on her face had him wanting to take it back.

Maggie took a step back from Jason and lowered her eyes to the ground. "I see," she said quietly. Reaching beyond him, she gently hit the button for the lobby and was relieved when they started moving. "I'm sorry if I did anything to make you uncomfortable, Jason. That was never my intention."

With a growl of frustration, Jason reached out and hit the stop button himself and then caught Maggie by the arms when the elevator car jerked to a halt. "Maggie, look at me," he said gently. When her eyes met his, they were wary and sad, and Jason felt like a schoolyard bully. "It wasn't *you*, okay? I just think it's better for us to stay focused on the project because when I let my guard down..."

Maggie couldn't help it, she leaned into him. "What?" she whispered.

Jason was only human. The feel of her, the smell of her perfume, and those big brown eyes looking up at him were his undoing. "I find it hard to forget that I shouldn't do things like this." And he lowered his mouth to hers. Maggie responded to him instantly and Jason thought he was going to lose his mind. Her lips were so soft, so pliant, and when she let out a sigh and relaxed into him, he took a step forward and pressed her back against the wall of the elevator.

He feasted on her lips like he'd been dying to for weeks as Maggie ran her hands up his neck and into his hair, anchoring him to her. Jason's tongue teased at Maggie's bottom lip and when she opened for him and touched her tongue to his, he thought he'd go up in flames. Jason wanted to tell her how much he wanted her, how much he'd been thinking about her and how he wanted nothing more than to cancel their meetings for today and go back upstairs when...

"Is everyone okay in there?" A voice was speaking to them through an intercom in the elevator and they broke apart instantly.

"Um...yes," Jason stammered. "We're fine." He reached

over and set the elevator in motion again. "Thank you," he said out loud to whoever was speaking to them, knowing there was probably a camera that caught all of that on tape. There was no way to claim a mechanical issue. They'd just have to step out into the lobby and pray that no one said anything.

They arrived on the main floor of the hotel and walked out to the waiting car. As they pulled away from the curb, Jason spoke without looking directly at Maggie. "I'm not going to apologize for that," he said simply.

"I'm not asking you to," she replied. There was so much that she wanted to say and that she wanted to ask, but now was completely not the time. They were wrapping up this trip and had two important clients to meet with today.

The timing of all this really sucked.

"So," she began, getting her head back where it belonged, "Dennis Caprese is up first this morning. I've talked to his assistant several times in the last couple of days and per all of your preliminary talks with him, I've prepared the contracts already, so that should everything go our way, he can sign today."

Jason nodded. He didn't give a damn about business and meetings right now. All he could think about was that kiss. Shouldn't she be outraged? Shouldn't she be demanding he not touch her again? He had been speculating for far too long about her marriage, and it just didn't sit right with him that Maggie wasn't putting up more of a fight. It didn't fit. The woman he had come to know had morals and was pretty traditional in her views and beliefs. It didn't match up with the image of her as a married woman. Jason had no doubt that she wasn't the kind of woman who would have an affair.

Then why did she kiss him with such urgency?

Why did it feel like she would gladly have let him take her right there in the elevator, and to hell with the consequences?

And why did he want to tell the driver to turn the car around so that he could test that theory out?

"Here we are, sir," the driver said, interrupting his thoughts. "I'll stay close by so you can call me when you're done."

Jason mumbled a word of thanks and exited the car, Maggie close behind him. All of his wonderings and naughty thoughts would have to wait. They had meetings to get through. But once business was done, so was all the tippy-toeing he'd been doing.

Jason was going to get some answers.

Tonight.

Their second meeting was over by four, but Alan Cummings, the CEO of AC Industries, invited them out for dinner. Jason had wanted to refuse, but Cummings wasn't one hundred percent on board yet and he figured that a few more hours in the man's company could only help their situation.

Maggie assumed Jason would send her back to the hotel to get started on paperwork and was surprised when he told Alan they'd both be there. Maggie looked at him quizzically, unsure why he wanted her to go with him when there was a mountain of work to do. Jason read the question in her eyes and simply said, "There will be plenty of time to get it all done when we get back to North Carolina."

She wanted to argue that she needed to get started while it was all fresh in her mind, but the reality was she really needed a little time away from Jason. After the kiss they'd shared earlier, he seemed to fill all the space around her. She could feel him, smell him, and found it hard to concentrate with him so close by.

But she didn't say a word. Instead, Maggie merely nodded and stayed put in the conference room of AC Industries until it was time to leave. "Do you need to go back to the hotel before dinner?" Jason asked.

"I wouldn't mind doing that, but it's completely up to you. Mr. Cummings seemed set on an early dinner so I don't think it would be worth the rush to go across town and back again."

"Apparently he does a dinner like this once a month with several clients, so we won't be one-on-one with him. I guess if nothing else, I may get to network a little more," Jason said casually.

"That would be great, Jason, but then maybe it would be best if I didn't go. I'll only be in the way, and no one else will have their assistants with them, so..."

"Nonsense!" Alan Cummings said as he walked back into the room. He was a tall man with a booming voice, and Maggie nearly fell out of her chair at the sound of it. "I have a couple of other out-of-town clients meeting us tonight and several of them have their assistants with them. And even if they didn't, Maggie, I would hate to not be a proper host and not include you."

She smiled at him but still didn't feel up to spending any more time talking about business. A little alone time back in her room to unwind and think about what had happened earlier in the elevator was what Maggie most wanted to do, but clearly that wasn't going to happen. "Thank you," she said finally, and stood when he indicated that they were ready to go.

Back in the town car, they rode over to a restaurant on the water where AC Industries hosted their monthly events. Maggie loved the sound and smell of the ocean and wanted nothing more than to kick her shoes off and go down on the sand to enjoy the feel of it between her toes. Unfortunately, Alan and Jason were waiting for her, so she smiled sheepishly and walked with them into the restaurant.

Within an hour, her head was spinning. They had met well over two dozen new people, had enjoyed hors d'oeuvres and several glasses of wine. All she wanted to do was sit down to a hot meal and finish the day, but Jason was working the room, deep in conversation. There was no way for her to get his attention and ask to leave without seeming rude.

Finally, dinner was announced and they were seated at a table for eight. It was some of the best seafood Maggie had ever tasted. Jason inquired if she was enjoying her meal, but once his eyes met hers, for the first time since the elevator, all thoughts of food left her mind. The heat in his eyes clearly matched her own, and it was all she could do to nod her head. "Everything's delicious," she whispered.

Jason stared at Maggie's lips and thought of how delicious they had been earlier in the day. He suddenly found himself without an appetite for food, ready to be done socializing. They had an early morning meeting with one last client and then an afternoon flight home. He needed to get through this last night and right now, all Jason wanted to do was take Maggie by the hand and drag her back to the hotel and to hell with the consequences.

"Jason!" Alan Cumming's voice shouted from across the room. He turned and faced the man. "There's someone here I want you to meet!"

With a sigh of resignation, he excused himself and

stood, but not before giving Maggie an apologetic look. She smiled serenely back at him; she understood. Once he was across the room and swallowed up into the crowd, she decided to take advantage of the time and walked out onto the back deck of the restaurant that led out to the beach. There were several other guests mingling out there, so she knew no one would pay too much attention to her.

Once outside, the sound of the waves crashing and the view of the sun setting were just overwhelming. Unable to resist, she headed down the wooden steps that led to the sand below, kicked off her shoes, and started toward the water. It felt better than she had imagined. She couldn't remember the last time she had been to the beach, and it was just heavenly to stand still and let her senses take it all in.

"I see that you've loosened up some, Mags," a voice said from behind her, and Maggie froze.

No, it couldn't be! Slowly, she turned around and gasped in horror. There, standing before her, was her former boss, Martin Blake.

"Martin," she said as calmly as she could, even though she felt as though she was about to be sick.

"I see you're still giving the come-on to your boss," he said snidely. "Tell me, will you go back to the hotel and cry foul again?"

She wanted to punch him in his smug face. "There's nothing to cry foul about," she said crisply. "I finally work for a man who knows the difference between someone being polite and someone issuing a come-on." She was rewarded when his expression faltered slightly. "Plus, I haven't had to fight my way out of a locked room to get away from someone who is no better than a rapist."

Martin's expression turned to pure fury. "You little

bitch," he sneered. "You led me on for months and then you had the audacity to run out and play the victim?"

"I *was* a victim," she fought back. "I never led you on; I never wanted you to touch me. *Ever.* You're disgusting and I hope never to see you again." She spat the words at him and then turned and walked away with her head held high until she was around the front of the restaurant. Then she nearly crumpled to the ground. Her heart was racing and she felt ready to retch.

Never in a million years had she expected to see Martin again, and right now, all she wanted to do was get in the car and leave. But she'd have to find Jason first. The thought of going back inside and chancing another run-in with Martin was overwhelming. She gulped in several breaths and tried to calm herself.

"Maggie?"

Suddenly, Jason was standing in front of her and gently pulling her to her feet. "What happened? Are you okay? Are you sick?"

She had never been so grateful to see anyone in her life. Well, that wasn't completely true. The last time she had felt this way, it had been William Montgomery saving her. "Can we leave?" she asked a little too urgently, clutching the front of Jason's shirt for support. "Please?"

"Of course," he said, and pulled her into his embrace. "What happened?"

"I don't want to talk about it right now. Can we please just go?"

Jason pulled back and looked down at her face. She was pale and her eyes glistened with unshed tears. Something was wrong. Something had happened, and while he wasn't going to push her right this minute, he knew he wouldn't rest until he found out. He led her to their waiting car and they rode back to the hotel in silence. Once inside, he let Maggie walk to the elevator while he headed to the concierge desk and ordered some tea to be sent up to her room.

He joined her moments later, and when they arrived up on their floor, he took the room key from her, opened her door, and followed her inside. Jason could be patient when he needed to be, but right now he felt anything but. He stood back and watched as she kicked off her shoes and placed her purse and briefcase on her desk before collapsing in the oversized chair next to the window.

"Maggie?" he asked softly. "What happened back there? Did someone upset you?" By now he had figured out she wasn't sick. There'd been no signs of that on the ride back to the hotel, so his next thought was that someone had caused this. "You can trust me, Maggie," he said when he saw the hesitation on her face.

"Three years ago, your father saved my life," she said in a voice devoid of emotion. "I worked for a big company as an executive assistant and I was away at a conference with my boss." Maggie stared out the window. "I had no idea that my boss had no real interest in the conference; he had brought me there to seduce me."

Jason felt fury rising inside of him. He tried to think of every face he had seen tonight and figure out who had done this to her. His thoughts were interrupted when she continued to speak.

"I was so naïve. I honestly had no idea what was going on. He had booked all the travel arrangements when that was normally my job, and instead of questioning it, I was thankful to have had one less thing to do." She grew silent for a moment and collected her thoughts before going on. "We arrived in California and I was so excited because I had never left the East Coast. When we got to the hotel, he checked us in. Again, I didn't see anything wrong with that. I had never gone on a business trip before, so to me, it was all completely on the up-and-up."

"Maggie, you don't have to..."

She faced him briefly. "No, it's okay, Jason. I want you to know." Maggie turned to look back out the window again. "It wasn't until we got up to the room and he closed the door behind me that I realized that something was wrong. He was so quick; one minute we were talking business and the next all of my personal belongings were snatched from me. He laughed and said how he'd been planning ways to get me alone for months. I tried to leave; I was clawing at the door as he was clawing at me. When I finally got free, he told me that if I went to the management or to the police, he'd tell them it was a lovers' spat and that I was black-mailing him for money. I knew they'd believe him over me. After all, he was a big-time executive and I was a nobody."

"That's not true, Maggie," Jason protested, but she wasn't listening.

"So, I left the room and got down to the lobby and real-ized I had no place to stay, no money, and no ID. That's when your father found me. He was so nice." She stopped and smiled at the memory. "I was so scared and he just sat with me in the lobby on the sofa and told me about himself, about his family, and then he offered to buy me a cup of coffee. He showed me his ID. By the time we were done with coffee, he had worked out a way to get my belongings back and offered me a chance at a new life and a new job."

Jason couldn't help but smile. That was his dad. William Montgomery took care of others and it was just one of the reasons why people loved him. He thought back to his first meeting with Maggie and how he had sensed that there was more to the relationship between her and his father, and now he understood it.

Standing, Maggie walked over to her mini fridge and pulled out a drink for each of them. Jason waved her off. "I asked the concierge to send up some tea for you. It should be here any minute."

She smiled sadly at him. "You are so much like your father, Jason," she said softly. "You take care of people."

"I only hope that I can be like him. Dad's an incredible man."

"You're more like him than you think." They were interrupted by a knock at the door and Jason walked over and let the uniformed server in. He set up the tray with tea and an assortment of fresh fruit and cookies on the table. Jason tipped and thanked him and then went back toward Maggie. She poured them each a cup and they sat in silence for several minutes, each absorbing all that had been revealed.

"He was there tonight?" Jason finally asked, breaking the silence. "Your former boss?"

She nodded slowly. "Yes."

"Did he speak to you?"

Maggie nodded. "When Alan called you over after dinner, I went outside and walked down to the beach. I just wanted a few minutes to feel the sand between my toes." She gave a mirthless laugh. "I never heard him approach. I was just standing there enjoying the sunset and the ocean breeze, and then there he was. He asked if I was going to lead you on back at the hotel and then cry foul."

"Son of a *bitch*," Jason muttered and then stood and began pacing the room. "Why didn't you come and get me?"

"There wasn't time. Plus, I had to face him, Jason. I have been hiding for three years. I never saw him again after your father found me in that lobby. If I was ever going to be free of this... this nightmare, I had to face him. I did my best, I really did. I held on to my dignity and didn't let him bully me, and then I walked away with my head held high. By the time you found me, I just crumpled. I held it together as long as I could." She let out another mirthless laugh. "Turns out that was about three minutes."

Her voice broke on the last word and then the tears finally fell. Jason was instantly at her side and he pulled her close. For the first time in three years, Maggie finally let herself cry openly in front of another person. Maybe now it would finally be over. Maybe now she wouldn't have to feel like an idiot. Or a victim. She had gotten away from Martin before he could do anything, and she knew now that she had done nothing wrong. It was a relief. She had let him have three years of her life, and now she was free.

She cried into Jason's shirt, and when she realized what she was doing and made to pull away, he simply held her closer. "Your shirt," she whispered.

"Don't worry about my damn shirt," he said gruffly as he led her over to the bed. Gently, he sat her down and then went over and closed the drapes. "I think you've had enough today. A good night's sleep will help a little, I hope." He smiled down at her. She was still dressed in her black pencil skirt and white blouse, but her hair was mussed up from her walk on the beach and all that had happened afterward, and her makeup was practically gone, and yet she was still the most beautiful woman he had ever seen.

"Sleep in tomorrow. I can handle the Hardwell people on my own," he said as he took a step away from her.

"That's not necessary," she protested and stood up. "You hired me to do a job and..."

"To hell with the job, Maggie!" he snapped, and then

cursed himself when she winced. She'd had a traumatic night and yelling at her wasn't helping. He took a calming breath. "Look, it's just that I know you've had an emotional night and I want you to rest and relax. I don't want you to have to be looking over your shoulder in case this guy shows up anyplace else, okay?"

She nodded, and Jason took a step toward her and gave her a gentle shove to make her sit down again. "Try to get some sleep, Maggie," he said softly.

"I doubt I'll get much sleep. If I close my eyes, I'll just see him," she said sadly. "I'm probably going to channel surf for a while."

Jason sat down beside her on the bed and took her hand in his. "You have to at least try to sleep."

Maggie turned to him and gave him a weak smile before shaking her head. "It took months before I was able to close my eyes and not see his face after it happened. I'd sleep with the TV on just so that I wouldn't hear his voice in my head."

"Where was your husband during all of this?" Jason asked, although he really didn't want to know.

Maggie didn't understand the question at first. Husband? What husband? In all the turmoil, that little white lie had been forgotten. How was she supposed to respond? What would a husband do? "Um, we weren't married yet, but whenever I let it get to me, he would just hold me until I fell asleep." She hoped that's what husbands did, but right now, she couldn't find the strength to care.

Jason nodded and released her hand. A million thoughts were racing through his mind, but first and foremost, he wanted to be the one to hold her until she fell asleep tonight. It was beyond inappropriate, and he knew he could never voice that out loud. Maggie had been through enough tonight with her previous boss without having to worry about her current boss harassing her, too.

"I wish there was something I could do or say right now to help," he admitted. "I don't think I've ever felt so helpless in my life. Thank you for trusting me with this, but I have to tell you, I want to know who it is and go after him and beat him senseless for what he's done to you!"

He stood and was about to walk away when Maggie reached out for his hand and pulled him back to her. "That won't help anything, Jason."

"Maybe not, but I know I'd feel a lot better. It sounds like there were no repercussions for this guy after what he did. I'd love to be the one to make him pay."

"Jason..."

He let out a long breath. "I get it. I do. I know it won't solve anything. I just..." He paused again. "I just can't bear the thought of you hurting like this and knowing I'm partially to blame."

Slowly, she shook her head. "It's not your fault, but I have a feeling no matter how many times I say it, you're not going to believe it. However, I really should thank you."

His eyes went wide with disbelief. "For what? For making you go to that damn dinner? You said you didn't want to go and I forced you. I could have let the car take you back to the hotel, but I didn't. I was selfish and unreasonable, and..." He let out a small growl of frustration. "That means it's my fault this happened! Do you know how that makes me feel?"

She knew exactly how he felt, because it was written all over his beautifully expressive face. Without thinking, she reached out and cupped his face in her hands. "Jason, I told you, you have nothing to be sorry for." She held her gaze steady with his, willing him to see how sincere she was. "No one could have predicted this happening."

"But..."

"In a million years, I never would have thought I'd run into him again. I've managed to steer clear of him for over three years. It was a really unfortunate coincidence that we ended up at the same place tonight." She shrugged. "The good news is that I was able to walk away this time before anything back happened."

He groaned as he said her name.

"Please don't let this eat at you the way it's been eating at me. He's not worth it and really, I'm fine. I was freaked out and I know I definitely panicked and thought I was going to be sick, but... you saved me." Pausing, she smiled sadly. "Thank you for being there when I needed someone and thank you for sitting here with a near-hysterical woman and calming her down."

Jason reached up and placed his hands over hers before pulling them away from his face. Her touch was killing him. "I wasn't there when it really mattered," he said, his voice gruff with emotion.

"You're here now," she whispered. Her heart was beating erratically as she studied his face. It would be easy to say thank you one more time and wish him a good night, but that's not what she wanted. She was brave once tonight, could she possibly be that brave again? Taking a steadying breath and letting it out slowly, she decided that she could. "And I don't want you to go."

He stared down at her and Maggie could read all the questions racing through his mind. She wouldn't blame him if he left, one of them had to be the voice of reason, right? But tonight, she seriously hoped they could put their working relationship in the corner and sort of forget about it. Instead of being boss and assistant, maybe they could just be a man comforting a woman.

"Maggie... I..."

"I don't want to be alone," she admitted. "I just want... I need..."

"What?" he asked so softly that she almost didn't hear him. "What do you need? Anything, Maggie. Anything you need, I'll do."

And she believed him.

With another steadying breath, she asked, "Will you hold me?"

As if she were made of spun glass, he carefully enveloped her in his embrace. "Yes," he whispered into her hair and she simply reveled in the feel of being wrapped in his arms.

"Stay with me tonight, Jason. Please."

He leaned back and looked down into her face. "I don't know if that's such a good idea."

She gave him a small smile, stepped out of his arms, and turned to pull down the comforter on the bed and turned out the bedside lamp. "I trust you, Jason." She sat down on the bed and reached for his hand. "I just need you to hold me."

He hesitated for the barest of moments before giving her a curt nod. Then he kicked off his shoes, removed his belt, and joined her on the bed.

There they lay, completely clothed, and clung to one another for the rest of the night.

EIGHT

JASON WOKE FIRST. They were still wrapped around one another as they had been last night, and he found that he could get very used to waking up with Maggie in his arms. Her hand was resting right over his heart; the hand that bore the ring of another man.

"Dammit," he whispered, and then gently tried to disentangle himself from her. Maggie let out a small sound of protest and when Jason was standing and looking down at her, her eyes fluttered open.

"What time is it?" she whispered.

"It's almost six," he said, trying hard not to let the anger he felt at himself show. When Maggie made to rise, he held up a hand to stop her. "Go back to sleep. It's early yet."

"I have to pack, and we've got the meeting at nine and..."

"I'm going alone. I told you that last night. You can stay here and pack. I'll send the car for you around eleven and we'll head to the airport."

"I can be packed in fifteen minutes, Jason," she countered. "There's no reason for me not to go with you." She rose from the bed.

With a huff of frustration, Jason took a step back. "This isn't up for discussion, okay? I'm telling you, as your boss, that I am going to this meeting alone. I want you to stay here and make sure that everything is packed up and ready to go when the car arrives."

As if the "boss" line wasn't enough, his tone said it all. It was clipped and sharp and was almost enough to make Maggie burst into tears. Again. "Fine," she said softly. "I'll make sure everything is taken care of." Before Jason could say another word, she stepped around him, went into the bathroom, and closed the door.

He took the hint.

Silently leaving the room, Jason walked across the hall to his own room. Once the door was closed behind him, he slumped against it and cursed himself. What the hell had he been thinking spending the night with Maggie? It was all innocent, but did it really make a difference? She was another man's wife and he had no right to spend the night in her bed. And the fact that she was his employee only made it worse.

Jason always considered himself a reasonable, level-headed man, and yet right now he was feeling anything but. He could go to this meeting this morning without Maggie and it wouldn't be a hardship, but what was he supposed to do once they were in the car together riding to the airport? Or flying home? Hell, what was going to happen once they got back to the office? How could he possibly look at her, spend time with her, knowing that he had crossed so many lines with her?

If her husband came and kicked his ass, he would take it. It was no less than he deserved. Jason had never gone after a married woman. He'd never even given one a second look. That was a line he never crossed. He believed in the sanctity of marriage and never wanted to be the cause of someone's marriage breaking up.

Until Maggie.

What was it about Maggie Barrett that had him breaking all of his rules? She was supposed to be the answer to all of his problems, but had ended up causing a whole lot more.

Jason dragged himself away from the door and went about packing. It would be good to get home and sleep in his own bed tonight. The thought of this trip finally being over was more of a relief than he ever thought possible. He needed to get his head back on straight, and maybe by the time they returned to the office on Monday, he would have an answer for how to work with Maggie *without* working with Maggie.

It was early and he was organized, so packing took little to no time and Jason found himself sitting on the edge of the still-made bed wondering what the hell to do next. Reaching for his phone, he decided that he needed to talk to someone.

And called the one person who would understand what he was dealing with better than anyone else.

"Somebody better be dead or dying for you to be calling this early," Lucas said sleepily into the phone.

"Good morning to you, too, Brother," Jason said, forcing the chipperness into his tone.

"Jason?" Lucas asked, coming a little more awake. "What's going on?"

"Look, I'm sorry to be calling so early in the morning but... I've got a situation on my hands and I need some advice."

"Give me a minute to get out of bed so I don't wake Emma," he said quietly, and Jason could hear the rustling of blankets as Lucas got up.

"I wouldn't have called so early if..."

"No worries, Jace," Lucas said. "Are you home already? Did everything go okay on the trip?"

"Everything is fine with the trip. We head home today after lunch."

"Okay, if it's not about the trip, then what's up?" Lucas asked around a very loud yawn.

Jason sighed. Where to begin? "You know how I've been having problems keeping an assistant ever since you and Emma hooked up?"

Lucas laughed. "You did make for some unforgettable stories. Personally, I thought that all the women would go after Mac; after all, he's the next in line to take over Montgomerys."

"What does that have to do with anything?" Jason snapped. "I'm the better looking one."

That only made Lucas laugh more. "Sure, you keep telling yourself that. Most women are looking for money *and* power. Mac has got that."

"I've got that," Jason mumbled.

"No, Brother, you're the typical middle child. You do your best to stand out and believe me, with two such spectacular brothers, I know it can't be easy for you!" Lucas was clearly having fun. It had been far too long since they'd just bantered like this.

"Why did I bother calling you?"

"Beats me, but believe me, I'd rather be back in bed with my beautiful wife than sitting here listening to you whine about... wait, what did you call about?"

"I was getting to that!" Jason snapped and then let out a

huff of frustration. "How did you deal with your feelings for Emma in the beginning? You know, with her working for us?"

"Wow..." Lucas began, "Um... okay. I don't know. I struggled with it. A lot. When we were snowed in at my place, that was the biggest hang-up for me. I mean, I didn't want to cross a line with her or have it come back that I had sexually harassed her or anything, but she let me know that it wasn't about work or Montgomerys. She was attracted to me."

"Yeah, but... when you both came back to work, wasn't it awkward?"

"Well, yeah, a bit, but that was because I still had the mind-set that I didn't want a relationship. I had to get my head on straight and I didn't want to drag Emma down with me. I was in love with her, but I thought it was better to stay away. Only I couldn't."

"Would you still have felt that way if Emma had been involved with somebody else?"

"Oh, shit, Jace... What have you done?"

"Nothing!" he replied defensively. "At least, nothing that bad."

"How bad?" Lucas asked.

"My assistant... Maggie?"

"Did you sleep with her?"

"No, not really..."

Lucas growled. "It's a yes or no question, Jace. Did. You. Sleep. With. Her?"

"Well..."

"Isn't she married? Wasn't that part of your criteria, that the person who went with you on this trip be married? How could you do that?" He let out a loud huff. "If Dad finds out about this..."

"I can't explain it, Lucas. That's why I'm calling you. It's a freakin' mess and I don't know what to do!"

"Start at the beginning and tell me everything that happened. I can't get you out of trouble if you leave crap out."

Jason told Lucas about their trip, from the kiss at the Rock and Roll Hall of Fame to their spending the night together fully clothed in Maggie's bed. Then he waited for Lucas to say something. After several tense and silent moments, Jason finally spoke. "Well? What am I supposed to do?"

Lucas let out a pent-up breath. "You need to talk to Maggie, man. You have to know what she's thinking. I mean, you can't just assume that you're both on the same page. A lot of what happened sounds like you were caught up in some weird moment and last night? Well, that was just a bad situation and it can all still be strictly platonic. But she's married, Jace. There's no way around that one."

"What do I do when we go back to work on Monday?"

"You're going to have to talk to her. If you're feeling awkward, chances are that she is too. She may not want to stay on as your assistant, but you can't just make that assumption and transfer her; you could be looking at some sort of human resources claim on that one."

Jason preferred to think that Maggie wouldn't go that route. Then again, he also preferred to think that Maggie wasn't really married, or was maybe in the process of leaving her husband, so his conscience could be clear.

"That is not a conversation I want to have," Jason admitted.

"Believe me, I didn't want to have to admit to Emma that I was afraid to get involved with anyone, but once the words were out, it was like a giant weight had been lifted." Lucas paused for a minute. "The thing is, Jace, I can tell you about me and Emma all day long. She wasn't a married woman. We were two single people who were attracted to one another. You and Maggie may very well be attracted to one another, but do you really want to pursue something with her? What about her husband? How would you feel if you found out some other man was hitting on your wife? And it was her boss? You can talk to her about where she'd be comfortable working, but I would strongly advise you not to pursue this relationship."

Jason knew his brother was right and he knew these were things he needed to hear. He had no idea how he was going to go about working with Maggie, seeing her every day and not acting on his feelings, but he was going to have to find a way.

"I know you're right, Lucas. I just needed to hear somebody say it out loud to me."

"I'm sorry, man. I know you were kind of hoping for someone to give you the okay to have your cake and eat it, too. But that's not going to be me. Hell, I hope it's not anyone. You need to get home and put an end to this."

"I will. And thanks, Lucas. I'm sorry I got you up so early."

"Don't ever apologize for calling when you're in need. Now if you'll excuse me, I'm going back to bed to kiss my beautiful wife awake and get on with my day."

"No need to brag," Jason mumbled.

"Hey, it's been a while since I had anything to brag about. I'm just making up for lost time."

It was hard to begrudge him that. They said goodbye, and Jason was left alone with his brother's words. It was now after seven and Jason knew he had to get ready for this last meeting and face Maggie and the decision he had to make.

~

Maggie had been ready and waiting in the hotel lobby at eleven o'clock when the car arrived for her. The driver informed her he had been scheduled to pick her up first and then go and get Jason. Once they had gone across town to pick him up, they were on their way to the airport.

"How did the meeting go?" she asked tentatively.

"Just as planned; he signed," Jason replied, checking his phone for voice mail or texts, anything to distract him from having to talk directly to Maggie. They drove in silence the rest of the way to the airport and checked in the same way.

By the time they were seated in first class for their flight home, Maggie had had enough. "Look, I know this trip has been difficult for you because of me, but I have had enough of the silent treatment!"

Jason turned and looked at her. "Excuse me?"

"Oh, please, you heard me just fine. I'm sorry I have been such a burden to you. I know you thought you had hired someone who was professional and had her life together, and instead you got stuck with me. I'm sorry I had a meltdown last night and I'm sorry I crossed a few lines with you. But we still have to work together and that's kind of hard to do with you ignoring me!"

He could only stare. *She* was taking responsibility for crossing lines? Didn't she realize he was crossing them just as much? "Maggie, you had every right to your meltdown last night and it was because of me that it happened!"

She held up a hand to stop him. "I don't want to spend the entire flight laying blame. All I'm saying is that I want to keep working with you, Jason, but I can't if you're going to act like this." Her brown eyes were wide and pleading, and Jason wanted to put her mind at ease.

"I wasn't sure you'd want to keep working with me," he finally said. "I know I put a lot on you during this trip and I didn't always act like I should have. I honestly don't know if our working together when we get back is for the best."

There, he'd said it; put the ball in her court.

Maggie continued to stare at him. "Oh," she said quietly, disappointment marking her features. "I guess you could be right. I'm sorry you feel that way. I thought I had done a good job for you and..."

"No, Maggie, it's not that you didn't do a good job. You did a great job! On everything! It's just that... we seem to have a problem working... together. Do you understand?"

She didn't want to, and so rather than continue with this uncomfortable conversation, she decided to change modes and pulled out her tablet to go over his morning meeting. If Jason had wanted to pursue their original conversation, he said nothing. They transitioned smoothly back into work mode and by the time they landed in North Carolina two hours later, Maggie felt confident that while she may not be working for Jason much longer, she had fulfilled her obligation to him and his father for this project.

They walked into the terminal. Maggie was determined to get to baggage claim and get home before she let herself cry. A strong hand on her arm halted her progress. "Maggie?" Jason said softly as she turned around to face him.

This was it, she thought. He's going to give me the speech now so that there would be no scene at the office on Monday. As much as she willed it not to happen, tears welled in her eyes. She took a deep breath in a feeble attempt to calm her nerves.

"I guess your husband will be here to pick you up," he said gruffly.

Her husband. She was getting damn tired of that lie hanging between them, but it was probably best to have that excuse to hang on to. "Yes, I'm sure he's waiting for me down in baggage claim."

Jason stared down into her face and swallowed the jealousy raging through him.

He wanted the right to take her home.

He wanted to tell her they didn't have to stop working together and be able to take her out on a non-work-related date.

He wanted... all the things he couldn't have.

"I just want you to know," he began, "that I couldn't have done this project without you."

She nodded her head, wishing he'd let go of her arm so she could walk away while her dignity was still intact. "I really need to go, Jason," she whispered.

"You never crossed any line with me, Maggie. That was all me. But I can't let you go before I say this."

"What?" she said, the words barely leaving her lips before his mouth claimed hers. Maggie quickly wrapped her arms around his neck and held Jason close to her. It was madness to be doing this in the middle of a crowded airport terminal, and yet she couldn't help herself. The kiss ended all too soon, and Jason stepped away.

"That's why we can't work together anymore," Jason said, his breath ragged. "I want you too much to work with you every day and not have the right to do that."

Maggie made to speak, but he stopped her. "Go, your husband must be waiting, and it looks like a storm is moving in. I'll feel better knowing that you got home safely."

Everything in her was clamoring to tell Jason the truth,

but she had to come to grips with what he had just admitted to. All this time, he had been just as attracted to her as she'd been to him! She reached up and stroked his cheek, unable to help herself, before turning and fairly running from him, disappearing into the crowd.

Jason meant to stay put and wait before heading down to baggage claim, but clearly, he was a glutton for punishment. Keeping a safe distance, he only wanted to catch a glimpse of what the man who was married to Maggie looked like. He watched as she collected her bags and then headed out the door and into the rain. Was he waiting for her in the car at the curb to keep her from getting wet?

Carefully, Jason picked his way through the crowd until he could look out the long expanse of windows and see Maggie walking outside. She flagged down a cab and climbed in while the driver loaded her luggage. Where was her husband? Why was she taking a cab? Why had she lied to him?

Taking out his phone, he dialed his father's number and then went to claim his own bags. When his father answered, he immediately launched into inquisition mode.

"I know all about what happened to Maggie when you met her three years ago," Jason said by way of greeting. "Why didn't you tell me?"

William didn't miss a beat. "It wasn't my place to tell you. When I hired Maggie to come and work for us, she asked that I not talk about it and really, there was never a reason to. How was the trip? I'm glad she felt comfortable enough to share that with you."

"She really didn't have a choice," Jason said with a bit of annoyance.

"Why? What happened?"

Jason relayed the events of the night before to his father.

"Dammit, I had hoped that she'd never have to see that bastard again. Is she okay?"

"She was pretty shaken up by the whole thing and by the time we got back to the hotel, she told me everything."

"I never meant to lie to you, Jace. It was all part of her requests when she came to work for us. Maggie never wanted to be put in that kind of situation again. Saying she was married just seemed to make her feel a little more... secure. I thought it was a crazy idea, but if it made her..."

"Wait, wait, *wait*!" Jason interrupted. "Maggie's not married?"

Uh-oh. "I thought you said Maggie told you every-thing?" William said, sounding a bit sheepish at letting the cat out of the bag.

"She told me everything about her ex-boss, not about lying about being married!" he yelled. "Geez, Dad! How could you not tell me?"

"You were demanding someone who was married to go with you on this trip! Maggie fit the bill!"

"But she wasn't really married!" Jason countered, not caring that he was getting looks from people around him in the airport.

"The lie served a purpose. Maggie was perfect for the position, but you didn't want a single woman. She didn't want to work for someone who was going to hit on her and that she couldn't feel safe with. It was what was best for everyone!"

"Dammit, Dad... do you have any idea..." Jason stopped as it all finally fell into place.

Maggie wasn't married.

They had done nothing wrong.

There was no husband.

"Jason? Are you there? Is everything all right?" his father asked frantically.

"I have to go. I'll talk to you over the weekend," was all he said before hanging up. Jason raced from the terminal and out to long-term parking. He was soaked to the skin by the time he arrived there. Throwing his luggage into the trunk, he quickly unlocked the doors and climbed in. Now he just had to figure out where to go.

Whipping out his phone again, he quickly called the office and got Ann on the phone. "Hey, Jace! How was the trip?"

He had to be careful to keep his tone neutral or Ann would know that something was wrong. "It was long and exhausting. We landed about a half an hour ago and unfortunately, I have one of Maggie's bags. Do you have her address so I can drop it off at her place? She already took a cab home."

"Oh, no problem..." Within a minute, Jason had the address and was programming it into his GPS and was on his way.

He drove like a man possessed. He'd been torturing himself for weeks for nothing. She had lied to him about being married. There had been nothing to feel guilty about because there was no husband. Each time he said those words in his head, Jason's heart beat a little bit faster.

Maggie was free.

They hadn't crossed any lines.

Not really.

There was still the whole boss and assistant thing to

work through, but that was nothing compared to what he thought they were dealing with.

There was nothing stopping them from exploring what had clearly begun on their trip.

Within twenty minutes, he was pulling into the parking lot of the apartment complex where she lived. There were no spots near her unit and he had to park at the far end of the lot, but it didn't matter. Right now, he'd run as far as he had to just to get to her. Hell, he'd run a damn marathon if she was the prize waiting at the end.

The rain was coming down in torrents, and he'd be lucky to get through this without catching pneumonia. Maggie's apartment was on the second floor and Jason took the stairs two at a time and soon found himself breathlessly pounding on her door. His heart was racing and he was physically shaking with nervous energy, but there was no way he was going to wait another minute to confront her about this.

Maggie opened the door a moment later and seemed genuinely shocked to see Jason standing there, staring at her and completely out of breath. "*Jason?* What are you...?"

"There's no husband," he said sharply and watched as she paled.

"What?"

"There. Is. No. Husband. Do I have that right?"

Maggie looked up at him, eyes wide. Then she seemed to realize what was happening and her expression turned to resignation before she nodded. "No, there is no husband."

"Good," was all he said as he pushed his way into her home, pulled her into his arms, and kissed her.

NINE

WHAT FOLLOWED WAS MADNESS.

Jason pinned Maggie to the wall while he feasted on her mouth. The only thing that kept urging him on was the fact that she seemed to be right there, feasting along with him.

When he moved from her lips to kiss her jaw and then down the column of her throat, Maggie spoke. "I'm sorry I lied to you," she said, and then let out a moan of pure pleasure as he gently bit her. "I didn't think it would ever be an issue."

Jason lifted his head and stared intently down into her eyes. Without ever breaking contact, he reached down and took her left hand in his, pulled the fake wedding ring from her finger, and threw it across the room. "Do you have any idea how I've been berating myself for the thoughts I've been having about you?" he asked before lowering his head to go back to nipping and kissing her neck.

Maggie merely shook her head. "I didn't know, Jason," she rasped as his hands began to move from her waist upward. She'd dreamed about this moment, fantasized about Jason's hands on her, and yet it was nothing compared to the reality of it. "If it helps, I've been having thoughts about you, too," she admitted.

"Oh, yeah?" Jason asked, lifting his head once again before bending slightly to scoop her up and into his arms. "How about you point me toward your bedroom and we can compare notes?" His tone was serious, but his eyes were bright with mischief.

Maggie couldn't help but smile as she wrapped her arms around his neck. "Straight down the hallway, last door on the left."

In a flash, Jason had her in her bedroom and was laying her down on the bed. He stood and simply looked down at her, taking in the sight of her sprawled out on the champagne colored comforter. She was so beautiful. He couldn't believe he finally had permission to touch her and not feel guilty about it or have to stop himself before going too far.

He was going to go as far as he could; and his hands actually twitched with the need to touch her again. "I've thought about this for so long, Maggie. I need to know that we're on the same page here."

"I want you, Jason," she said honestly. "It almost killed me to leave the airport earlier."

It was all the encouragement he needed. He peeled his wet shirt off and let it drop to the floor before kicking his shoes off and removing his trousers and socks. Maggie leaned up onto her elbows to watch him. When Jason stood before her in nothing but dark briefs, she gave an appreciative smile.

Silently, she stood and slowly unbuttoned her own plain white blouse, adding it to the pile Jason had begun. Reaching behind her, she unzipped her skirt and let it fall to the ground, leaving her in nothing but simple white lace. "Is this the page that you're on?" she asked, "Or am I missing something?"

Her words were meant to tease, but Jason was too on edge to play along. Jason lifted his hands and cupped Maggie's face. "I'm going to apologize right now for not taking the time to go slow. I need you, Maggie."

She gave him a sexy smile and stepped back, and lay down on the bed in invitation. "I don't care about slow, Jason," she said. "I just care about feeling you here beside me." She crooked a finger at him.

He didn't need to be asked twice.

It could have been days or it could have been hours, Jason wasn't sure. He was flat on his back, with Maggie wrapped around him as he tried to catch his breath. In his wildest fantasies, he'd never imagined how explosive they would be together. Once he had joined her on the bed, it was as if they had been two starving people who could finally eat.

He smiled at his own analogy because he had certainly feasted on every inch of Maggie's amazing body. She kept it pretty well-hidden underneath her conservative clothing, but now that he knew what was underneath, he could never look at her the same way again when they were in the office.

The room had darkened quite a bit, so Jason knew they'd been in there for hours. A quick glance around the room revealed a clock; it was nearing eight. He turned his head to the side and smiled at the sight of Maggie's head on his chest and her blonde hair in wild disarray.

"Hey," he said softly, and waited for her to raise her head. When she did, he asked, "Are you hungry?"

That wicked grin he was really beginning to love

appeared. "I could eat," she said simply and then gave a little shriek when he reached out and rolled her under him, pinning her to the mattress.

"Food, woman," he playfully snarled then he kissed her soundly. "You have worn me out. I need something to eat."

Maggie pushed him off and rose from the bed to grab a robe from her closet. "Well, obviously I don't have anything here since I've been gone for three weeks, but we can order some takeout," she suggested.

Minutes later, they were scrolling through one of the food delivery apps until they could agree on someplace. "Their pizza is pretty decent, but if you wanted something else like pasta, I'd say we should keep looking," she said of the one place Jason finally suggested. "I'm just glad there are services like this so we don't have to actually go out and pick dinner up. Although I do kind of feel bad about anyone having to go out in this weather."

The rain was still coming down hard and Jason took that as a sign she wouldn't want him going out in it either; hopefully that would include for the rest of the night. He wasn't ready to leave yet and he had a feeling it would be quite a while before he'd actually *want* to go home. Mentally shaking his head, Jason knew he'd have to wait and see what Maggie wanted. After all, they had been together non-stop for three weeks; she might want some time away from him.

True, they hadn't been sleeping together for three weeks, so maybe she wouldn't mind him being around while they explored this new aspect of their relationship.

Relationship? Normally that word had Jason breaking out in a cold sweat, but right now, it made him feel good. He already knew they were compatible at work and he genuinely enjoyed just spending time talking with Maggie.

The last couple of hours had proved they were compatible in bed, too. What more could he ask for?

"Is there anything else you want to add, or can I place the order?" Maggie asked as she studied the screen.

"Go for it. I think we ordered more than enough for the two of us." Jason reclined on the pillows, sheets draped over his hips, as he watched her. The last five weeks had been transforming. The woman he had met initially was uptight and prickly, and now he understood why. The thought of someone doing something so horrible to Maggie made his fists clench. If he had known who that lousy SOB was while they were at dinner last night, he had no doubt someone would have had to come and bail him out of jail, because he would have taken great delight in beating the man into the ground.

"They said about thirty minutes, but I'm thinking closer to forty-five in this weather," she was saying as she sat back down beside him. "I hate that I don't have anything to offer you to drink other than water." She blushed slightly. "Although, I should probably do an online grocery order too. It won't be here quite as fast as dinner, but..."

Sensing her discomfort, Jason reached out and pulled her down beside him so her head was back on his shoulder. "I can wait for the food to get here," he said softly, kissing the top of her head and sighing with contentment. When she didn't say anything, he gently shrugged his shoulder to get her attention. "What's going on, Maggie? Do you want me to go?"

She sat back up. "I don't want you to go, but I'm just a little... well, compared to the places that we've stayed, my place is a little... dumpy."

Jason reached out and placed a finger under her chin, forcing her to look up at him. "There is nothing wrong with your home. I don't give a damn where we are, Maggie. I just want to be with you."

That made her relax and smile. "I want to be with you, too, Jason. But I have to admit, you've spoiled me."

"Me? How?"

"I was thinking how it was going to be great to come home and sleep in my own bed, but after some of the luxurious hotels we stayed in, I realize this bed is old and not that comfortable."

He laughed and pulled her back down beside him. "I didn't even notice because I was perfectly comfortable having you wrapped around me."

"Still, you have to admit that a comfortable bed would be a nice bonus."

He made a noncommittal sound. "We may have to go back to some of those hotels and do a comparison." A slow smile crept across his face at the thought of going back to New York, being able to share a room with her, and doing all the things they had missed out on because it wouldn't have been appropriate. Carriage rides through Central Park or taking in a Broadway show after dining out at some exclusive restaurant all seemed perfect to him.

"I'll tell you what, I wouldn't mind going back for one of the pretzels we had in New York and maybe going to the Statue of Liberty," Maggie said as if reading his mind.

Jason let out a small laugh. "I was just sitting here thinking about how I'd like to take you back to New York to see a show or maybe to eat at some fancy restaurant and you're talking about pretzels. It's funny!"

She playfully punched him in the arm. "I don't care about the fancy stuff, Jason. That doesn't impress me. I had fun running around the city and taking in the experience; meeting people, tasting the food... it was all just so amazing!

I'll never be able to thank you enough for giving me that day. It was perfect and I'll never forget it."

Her words were so sincere, and the look in her eyes told Jason more than anything how much it all had meant to her. In that moment, he vowed to himself to take her back there and give them the time to do what they wanted at their leisure; no time limits or constraints, just the chance to enjoy themselves and relax.

"You're very welcome. Someday we'll go back and play at being the ultimate tourists," he said and kissed her again. It would have been easy to keep kissing her and perhaps sneaking in another round of making love to her, but he was curious about what she'd most like to go back and see.

"Oh, there's just so much," she said before talking about some of the sites she would be interested in. He loved talking to her, and it didn't matter what the topic was.

They talked about food and some of the Broadway show signs they'd seen and which ones they'd be most interested in going back and seeing. He was just settling in, enjoying the feel of Maggie relaxing against him, when they heard the doorbell ringing.

"Don't take this the wrong way," Maggie said as she jumped from the bed, nearly giddy, "but I'm so excited that dinner is here!" She bolted from the room, and Jason could hear her laughing as she went to open the door.

He climbed from the bed and winced as he reached for his still damp pants. It was not at all appealing to put them back on, so he wrapped a sheet around his middle, scooped the clothes up off of the floor, and walked out to the kitchen, where he found Maggie setting their food down. "Would you mind if I tossed these in the dryer? They're still pretty wet."

Maggie took the clothes from him, making sure the

pockets were empty, and tossed them in the dryer, turning to admire the sight of Jason wrapped in a sheet. Slowly she walked toward him and placed her hand over where he was holding the sheet together. "Nice outfit," she said saucily, and got up on tippy-toes to place tiny kisses along his chin. "You look good in my sheets."

Jason let out a low growl as her hands wandered over his chest, his shoulders, and his arms. "You think so?"

Maggie nodded. "I do. But..." She reached back down and pulled his hand away from its makeshift fastening. "I think I like you much better out of them." In a flash, the sheet dropped to the tile floor.

"What about dinner?" he asked and groaned as she began to kiss her way down his body.

"That's what microwaves are for," she said.

The rain had stopped by the next morning and Jason's clothes were long since dried. He could very easily go out to his car and grab his luggage so he had something clean to wear, or he could go home and unpack and let Maggie get herself settled back in. But...

He didn't want to leave.

The thought of going home to his big, empty house left him cold. He'd bought the big townhouse on the golf course because it suited his needs. But now? It just seemed like a place that was way too big for a man alone. Maggie stretched beside him and then snuggled closer. She was a snuggler, and Jason found that he enjoyed it.

Unfortunately, the thought of cold pizza for breakfast was not doing it for him, and he knew it would be best for him to get up and go and get them breakfast and for them to talk about how they were going to spend their day. It was funny because he thought after spending so much time together that he'd be ready for some time alone, but he wasn't. If anything, now that he knew that there wasn't any reason for them not to be together, he didn't want them to be apart.

"I can hear you thinking from here," Maggie said sleepily, yawning. "What time is it?"

"Almost nine," he said. "I was thinking about breakfast. Then I was thinking about clean clothes and my luggage. And then..."

"Then you were thinking about going home," she said quietly and sat up beside him. "It's okay for you to leave, Jason. I don't expect you to move in or anything just because we slept together."

"Do you want me to leave?" he asked, sitting up beside her.

She huffed with frustration. "Please don't answer my question with a question. It's annoying. All I'm saying is I know that you have a life to get back to. Obviously, you didn't go home after we landed yesterday, and just like I've got things to do around here to get settled back in before we have to go back to work on Monday, I'm sure you have things to do at your place. It's okay."

He leaned in and kissed her squarely on the mouth. Short and sweet. "I know I have stuff to do, but I just wasn't ready to... leave yet."

That made Maggie smile. "I'm not kicking you out."

"That's good," he said, and his smile matched hers. "But I am hungry and leftover pizza is not what I want for breakfast. How about I go and get us some bagels and coffee or something?"

Maggie shook her head. "I know you'd never know it

after all the breakfasts we've shared in the last month, but normally I am not a breakfast person. I think I gained a good five pounds just from the breakfast foods. I'm kind of anxious to shower and get laundry going and then hit the grocery store. Monday will be here before you know it."

He nodded in understanding. "Can I take you to dinner tonight?"

She blushed and her smile grew. "I would like that very much."

"That's good. I want to take you out someplace nice and not talk about business and not have to share you with anyone."

"You don't have to make a fuss, Jason. I'd be happy just going someplace casual."

He knew she would put up an argument, but he also knew that for one night, he wanted to spoil her a little. "You'll just have to wait and see," he said distractedly.

"How will I know what to wear?" Maggie asked, leaning in to trail kisses down the column of his throat to his sculpted chest.

"Whatever you wear, Maggie, will be perfect."

She raised her head and looked at him doubtfully.

Jason whipped the sheet away from them both and scooped her up into his arms. "Personally, I can't wait to see you wearing nothing but bubbles..."

He arrived back at Maggie's promptly at seven. "Wow," he said, stepping inside and handing her a bouquet of white tulips. "You look absolutely beautiful."

She blushed. All day she had worried about what to

wear, because Jason had essentially seen most of her wardrobe over the last several weeks, but then she remembered a cocktail dress she hadn't had the opportunity to wear.

Now, dressed in the curve-hugging black dress with the tiny straps and wearing a pair of killer skinny heels, Maggie knew she had made the right choice. "Well, I wasn't sure where we were going, so I decided I couldn't go wrong with a little black dress."

He leaned in and kissed her, slowly and thoroughly, and when he lifted his head, he scanned her slumbrous and sexy eyes and smiled. "It's perfect."

She turned and grabbed her purse and a wrap to take with her and then walked out the door that Jason was holding open for her. "Are you going to tell me where we're going?"

"We'll be there soon enough," was all he said as he placed a strong hand on the small of her back and led her over to his sporty BMW.

Within minutes, they were in downtown Charlotte and pulling up in front of one of the best steakhouses in the state. Maggie was more than a little impressed with Jason's choice and then heard a commotion across the street. A sports bar. She sighed wistfully and jumped when Jason called her on it.

"Is there a hockey game on tonight?" he asked with a knowing smirk.

"I don't know... maybe."

Indecision marked his face. On one hand, he wanted to take her out for a romantic dinner where it was just the two of them and he could spend time getting to know her. Then he remembered how much fun she had when they had gone to see the game at Madison Square Garden. His mind made up, Jason walked around the car, took Maggie by the hand, and began leading her across the parking lot.

"Jason? The restaurant is back there."

"Yeah, but you know you'd rather be over here watching the game and eating a burger," he teased and was surprised when Maggie stopped short and stood her ground. He turned and faced her. "It's not a big deal. As long as I'm with you, I don't care where we eat."

She closed the distance between them and kissed him. "I can watch the game later on the DVR. I'd very much like to have a quiet dinner, just the two of us."

Nothing could have pleased him more. They walked back toward the restaurant and were seated immediately at a quiet corner table. Maggie was overwhelmed by the atmosphere and the menu, but it didn't take long for her to relax and order. When all the preliminaries were out of the way, Jason reached across the table for one of her hands. "Thank you for coming out tonight."

"Thank you for inviting me." She looked around and sighed at the beautiful surroundings. "So, tell me," she began, "do you think we accomplished everything that you wanted on this trip?"

"Oh, no. No talk about business tonight. Tonight, I want to learn more about you," he said seriously, his thumb gently stroking her knuckles. "I want to know about your family, where you grew up and... everything."

She blushed as she ducked her head on a chuckle. "That's quite a list. I grew up in Virginia and went to college at the University of Richmond. My parents are great; they're retired now and down in Florida."

"Why didn't you say anything? We could have stopped to see them," Jason said, concern marking his handsome features.

"Jason, we were working *and* on a tight schedule. Believe me, there is no such thing as a quick visit with my family. I don't see them as much as they'd like, and so whenever I do plan to visit, it's for at least a week. Anything less and I get the huge guilt trip."

"If my dad ever retires and he and Mom move away, I think we'll have to deal with the same thing. Working with Dad ensures that we see him every day, and Mom stops in enough that we see her several times a week. I think it would be strange not to see them so often."

"You get used to it," she said and reached for her water. "Luckily, I have older siblings who are each married and keep my parents entertained with grandchildren. As the baby of the bunch, I get a little more smothering than they do, but they claim it's all out of concern."

"They just want to make sure you're okay and taken care of."

"Yeah, well, it's nice not to have them living so close by. When everything happened... three years ago, I didn't tell them. I didn't want them to worry, and as your father stepped in and took care of everything, all they needed to know was that I had gotten a fabulous job offer and jumped on it."

Jason nodded and then felt his rage building just thinking about her ex-boss again. "Maggie, I hate to bring up an uncomfortable subject, but I need to know. Was this guy at any of our meetings? Was he with any of the companies that we met with?"

She shook her head. "No, no... I hadn't seen him anywhere else and the company that he ran back in Virginia was owned by his brother-in-law. I doubt he left it. It was all just a terrible coincidence that he was there."

"Can I ask his name?"

Maggie's head snapped up and she looked at Jason in horror. "Why? Why would you even want to know?"

"If there is even the slightest chance this guy is doing business in the same circles as I am, I need to know who he is so Montgomery's doesn't do business with him. The last thing I want is to do business with someone who would treat a woman the way this creep treated you."

For a moment, she felt oddly deflated. Secretly, she had hoped Jason wanted to know the name so that he could track Martin down and defend her honor. It was a ridiculous thought, she knew, even so, it was easy to picture Jason in the role of knight in shining armor. "Martin Blake," she said quietly.

Jason simply nodded and quickly changed the subject. "So, two older siblings? Tell me about them."

Part of her was relieved that he would not pursue the conversation about Martin any further. Smiling, she took a sip of her water and launched into a funny story about growing up as the baby of a family of five.

TEN

BEING BACK in the office on Monday wasn't nearly as uncomfortable as Maggie had thought it would be. After debating extensively whether or not it would be wise to continue working together, ultimately neither one was ready to admit it wasn't a good idea. So it was with confidence that she walked through the executive office of Montgomerys and went about getting settled at her desk.

"Maggie!" William Montgomery's voice boomed from across the room. "You're back from your whirlwind trip. I saw from all the reports that it was a rousing success." He walked over and gave her a hearty embrace that made her smile. "Not that I expected anything less from you and Jace. I knew you would be the perfect assistant for him. So tell me, did everything go okay?"

She couldn't help the smile growing across her face. "Everything was wonderful. We met so many people, and while not all of them were a good fit for Montgomery's, we had some interesting stories to talk about afterward. Then there were the places we stayed and the things we saw... I got to stand next to John Lennon's guitar at the Rock and

Roll Hall of Fame! Then we went to see a hockey game at the Garden. Oh, it was just amazing!"

William couldn't help his own grin. He knew that pairing the two of them together was the right thing to do! While he couldn't be sure that anything had clicked romantically yet, from the exuberance in Maggie's voice and the spring in Jason's step, William could tell it was just a matter of time.

"I am so glad it went so well," he said when she finished talking. "I know you were worried about going on the trip, but it sounds to me like you had nothing to worry about. Jason would never do or say anything to hurt anyone."

"No, I know now that he wouldn't. You've raised an amazing son and I'm so glad I've had the opportunity to work with him and get to know him. You should be very proud."

"Believe me, I am. All of my boys are amazing, but it's nice to see that others see it as well."

She nodded.

"Well now, you're going to keep working together, aren't you? I mean, Jason still needs an assistant, and I can't imagine after all the interesting things you two managed on this trip that you'd be eager to go back to customer service."

"Actually, Jace and I talked about that and we're going to see how it goes. We still have a lot to do to wrap up all the dealings from the trip, and then we'll see if it's really necessary for me to stay up here."

"Nonsense, Jason has always had an assistant. Granted, he and Mac had Rose splitting her time between them for a while, but with all of this new growth, Jason's going to need his own assistant. Plus, I think Mac enjoys having an assistant of his own, too."

Maggie shrugged and gave a noncommittal, "We'll see,"

before reaching over and getting her computer booted up. "I hope you're right, but for now, I'm content to live in the moment and see where Jason needs me to be."

William smiled knowingly. "So, um... how did the whole husband thing work for you? Did you have to play the married card much?"

Maggie blushed. "Actually, it didn't come up too much while we were on the trip, but I ended up telling Jason the truth. I'm not sure how to go about doing that around here."

"No worries," William said. "I'll take care of it. We'll just tell people you've been legally separated for some time and now you're finally getting a divorce and would like everyone to respect your privacy."

"I can't ask you to do all of that for me again. I got myself into this mess, I'll get myself out."

William waved her off. "Maggie, it's worth it for me just to see you looking so happy and relaxed. I've never seen you smile so much. I hated pushing you into this trip, but I'm glad now that I did."

"Me too, sir," she said wholeheartedly. "Me too."

It was almost lunchtime when Jason finally had time to call Maggie into his office. From the moment he had gotten in earlier, he had been wrapped up in conference calls and returning messages, and then meeting with his father and brother to discuss all the contacts he'd made while he was away and where he saw all of this expansion going. His frustration level at not having a minute to himself was getting to him. Picking up his phone, he buzzed Maggie's desk and essentially barked for her to come into his office.

Less than a minute later, she was standing in his doorway, tablet in hand and looking anxious. "I wasn't sure what else you needed me to bring," she said nervously. "I left all the essential files on your desk while you were in with your father and brother."

"Come in and close the door, Maggie," he said sternly and while her back was turned, he quickly moved around his desk so he was right behind her when she turned around.

She nearly jumped out of her skin at the sight of him so close to her. "Oh, Jason! You scared me half to death." It was the last thing she got to say for a long time. Jason's mouth came down on hers and claimed her in a slow, wet kiss that went on and on and on. When he finally released her, Maggie sagged against him. "Oh, my..."

Jason reached up and cupped her face, taking in the flushed skin and bright eyes, and smiled. "Hey," he said softly.

"Hey, yourself. How is your day going?"

"Much better now that I have you to myself for a few minutes," he said, taking Maggie by the hand and leading her to the sofa to sit down. "How about you? How has your day been so far?"

They talked business briefly, and when Jason invited Maggie to join him for lunch, she hesitated. "I don't know, Jason," she said, chewing her bottom lip. "I don't think it's a good idea for us to be socializing here at the office."

"We're not; it's just lunch, Maggie. It's not a big deal."

"Trust me, it is. None of the other assistants go out with their bosses."

"Emma used to go out with Lucas all the time!"

"They're married; it's not the same thing."

Jason sighed with frustration. "Fine, I get it. You don't want anyone speculating on our relationship. I can respect that. How about dinner? Can I take you to dinner tonight?"

She smiled. "Actually, how about I make dinner for you? You can come by when you're done here and we'll just hang out and relax. What do you say?"

He narrowed his eyes at her. "Is there a hockey game on? Is that why you don't want to go out?"

Maggie couldn't help but giggle. "Maybe. Either way, after a long day back at work, I think it will be nice just to be able to relax and be casual and *maybe* catch a game on TV."

Jason leaned forward and kissed her on the nose. "Sounds good to me. I normally leave here around six so I could be at your place by six thirty. Will that work?"

"Perfectly."

When six thirty rolled around, Maggie was ready. She had the table set, a salad made, sauce simmering on the stove, and a pot of water ready to come to a boil for the pasta she had waiting to go. All she needed was Jason.

At six forty-five, she was mildly concerned, and by seven, she was on her way to being seriously pissed. She had put off calling Jason as long as she could and before she could let herself be genuinely angry, she needed to call him and make sure he wasn't hurt somewhere on the side of the road.

The fact that he answered and there were no sirens in the background confirmed he was perfectly intact.

For now.

"Oh, damn, Maggie..." he stammered distractedly. "What time is it?"

"It's seven o'clock. I was just wondering if something

came up or if you were still coming over." She tried not to come off sounding annoyed, but she didn't think she quite pulled it off.

"Um... yeah, I lost track of time. I got a call from the people we met with in Atlanta and it turned into a conference call and then I was going over some projections with Mac and we're trying to figure out."

"It's okay, Jace, really." She did her best to squash her disappointment. "It's not a big deal. It was just a quick dinner and some TV; no worries. We can do it another time."

He hesitated before responding. She heard him whispering, "Give me a minute," to Mac, she assumed, and then he spoke. "I really am sorry, Maggie. It's just that this project is so big and time consuming and it didn't all come to an end when we got back."

She wanted to yell that she knew that because she had been working on the damn project with him for weeks! But she held her tongue and spoke sweetly. "Jason, I knew from the get-go that your work is very important to you. I would never expect you to blow it off for me."

"Dammit, Maggie, you're important to me, too. I honestly lost track of the time. I'm sorry," he said sincerely. "If it's not too late..."

She smiled at his effort. "Jason, you're obviously in the middle of a bunch of stuff. Go back to it so you and Mac can actually go home tonight. I'll see you in the morning."

"But I wanted to see you tonight."

She could almost see the pout from the sound of his voice.

"Go back to work, boss," she said, ignoring his statement. "I'll see you in the morning. Good night."

He wished her a good night and wanted to say more,

but she had already hung up. Jason reclined in his chair, thinking about their conversation, when his brother came back into the office.

"Care to tell me why your assistant is calling you and what you were apologizing for?" Mac was the oldest of the Montgomerys, and far more serious than his younger siblings. If Lucas had made the statement, there would have been a hint of teasing; when Mac made it, it was an accusation. That had Jason's back up in defense.

"None of your damn business. Let me see that contract for Atlanta," he said, leaning over his desk toward the file in Mac's hand.

"Hell, no. I want to know what's going on, Jace. You've been distracted all day, walking around with a sappy grin on your face, and now Maggie's calling you after hours and... Oh, no... you didn't."

Jason merely glared at him. "Choose your next words carefully," he warned.

"After all your bitching and complaining about your previous assistants all hitting on you and you're sleeping with Maggie? What the hell's the matter with you?"

"Maggie is nothing like those other women," Jason defended. "And neither of us planned on this happening, it just... did."

"Geez, Jason, isn't she married?"

Jason hated to betray Maggie's confidence, but he felt it was best if his brother understood the whole story. By the time he was done explaining about her former boss and the way their father had saved her, Mac had visibly relaxed.

"I think you're making a mistake, bro," he finally said. "Sleeping with your assistant never ends well."

"It did for Lucas and Emma."

Mac swiped a hand over his face. "I honestly wish the

two of them had met some other way. I am tired of everything getting compared to Lucas and Emma. I mean, don't get me wrong, I am happy for them both, and Emma is terrific, but every time someone has a problem around here, it all comes back to the two of them and how everything worked out."

"This is different, Mac. I mean, I fought it, I really did, but there is just something about her that I can't explain. She's smart and funny and we have great—"

"Sex?" Mac teased.

"Watch it," Jason warned again. "I was going to say great conversations. She's exciting to be with."

"So, this is serious?"

"I think it could be," Jason admitted and found it wasn't such a hard thing to do.

"How does Maggie feel?"

"I'm not sure. We were supposed to have dinner tonight, and I'm sort of treading carefully with her because of her past. I don't want to rush her or do anything to scare her off."

"So then, what are you doing here with me working late when you had plans with her?"

Jason shrugged. "This is who I am; work has always been first and foremost in my life. Maggie knows that."

Mac laughed and shook his head. "Yeah, there's a difference between knowing your boss is a workaholic and dating a workaholic. You'll have to pay more attention to the time, Brother, otherwise, you may find that she's not as understanding as you thought."

Jason waved him off. "You don't know Maggie. She'll understand. But you're right. I will start paying more attention to the time and try to get out of here more often at a reasonable hour. How hard could it be?"

~

By the end of the week, Jason knew how hard it could be.

Damn near impossible, apparently.

He didn't realize how much of himself he gave to the business until there was something else that he wanted to do, and yet he couldn't tear himself away. Maggie had been patient all week long, always quick with a word of understanding.

It was Jason who hit the breaking point.

At six o'clock on Friday evening, Mac walked into his office and smirked. "Working late on a Friday night? Nice."

"Shut up," Jason snapped as he walked around collecting paperwork and shoving it into his briefcase.

"You've been here late every night this week," Mac said lightly. "How's that working for you?"

Jason flipped him the bird and closed his case, walking toward the door.

"Big plans tonight?"

Jason stopped and hung his head down. "Is there something you wanted, Mac?" he finally asked.

Mac was the king of poker faces, and he gave Jason his best *dude, I'm really sorry to have to do this to you* face. "Well, actually, I just needed to come in here and let you know," he paused for dramatic effect "that I'm glad you're finally taking your sorry ass out of here and hopefully going out with Maggie."

Jason was so relieved he practically sagged to the floor. "You're an idiot," he murmured as he turned and strode out the door.

"I do not want to see you back here until Monday!" Mac called after him.

By the time Jason got to his car, his brother was all but

forgotten. He had to get to Maggie. All day he had tried to pin down plans for them for tonight, but she had been elusive, telling him just to call her if he had the time. He hated letting her down. All week. He had had no time alone with her since that brief time in his office on Monday, and he was ready to explode with the need for her.

Looking at his phone, Jason thought about calling her and telling her he was on his way over, but he wanted to surprise her. After a quick detour to pick up flowers, he finally pulled in at Maggie's complex and, as he had the first time he'd come here, he sprinted up the stairs two at a time to get to her.

"Jason!" Maggie exclaimed when she opened the door to him moments later. "I thought you were going to call when you left the office."

Not quite the greeting he was hoping for, but he could work with it. "I had to see you," he admitted. "I didn't want to call and give you the chance to tell me not to come by." He handed her the bouquet of exotic flowers and waited for her to invite him in.

She didn't.

"Is... is this a bad time?" he finally asked.

"What? Oh, no... sorry. Bad manners. Come on in." She stepped aside as he walked in, and then she headed for the kitchen to find a vase.

Jason watched as she arranged the flowers, fluttering around the kitchen, and he wanted to just grab her and kiss her and make love to her all night long. Fortunately, he was smart enough to know that caveman tactics would probably not be appreciated right now. "Have you had dinner yet?"

"No, I haven't. I was planning on heating up some pasta and watching a movie." She waited a moment before asking, "Would you like to join me?"

A wicked smile crossed his face as he stalked her from across the kitchen. Without asking permission, he hauled her up against him and kissed her with all the pent-up passion and frustration he'd felt all week. Luckily, Maggie was ready for his sexy assault and wrapped her arms around him to keep him close.

Jason broke the kiss long enough to pick her up and haul her over his shoulder while she shrieked with laughter.

Maybe caveman tactics weren't such a bad idea after all.

"I'm really sorry about this week."

"It's okay."

"No, it's not," he said solemnly, hours later. They were naked and wrapped up in each other's arms, and it felt like everything was right in his world. "I never had a reason to clock out at five and I guess I should have been paying more attention to my work habits."

Lifting her head from his shoulder, Maggie smiled at him. "Look, I'm not going to lie to you, it bothered me that you kept blowing me off. It felt like once we finally... you know... slept together, that you were done. I wasn't expecting a proposal or for you to change your entire life for me, Jace." She shrugged. "I just really enjoy our time together."

"I do too, and I hated myself every time I looked at the clock and realized I'd let you down. I promise to do better. Next week, I..."

She immediately placed a finger over his lips. "Please don't make any promises. That will only upset us both when you break them."

He wanted to argue that he wasn't going to do that, that he had learned his lesson this week, but she was right.

Guiding her head back to his shoulder, he gently caressed her arm. "So, tell me how your week was."

"Hmm... well, my new boss is kind of a jerk, but..."

"Hey!" he said with a laugh. "Cheap shot!"

Grinning up at him, she stuck her tongue out before saying anything else. "But other than that, I'm enjoying the work. Rose has been incredibly helpful and I think I'm settling into a good routine."

He nodded. "That's good. So... no plans to go back to customer service?"

That made her laugh. "I hadn't thought about it recently, but now that you've mentioned it..."

"Maggie..."

"I'm kidding," she told him. "Now that I've had a taste of being back in an intellectually challenging position, I can't see myself ever going back. I'll admit that sometimes I feel a little out of my element with some of the programs, but that's what Rose has been working on with me. She has the patience of a saint, that woman."

"She must if she works with Mac. Even indirectly," he murmured.

"Oh, stop. I'm sure he's fine."

"Have you met him?"

"Actually, I haven't," she admitted. "None of the executives come down to customer service, so..."

"Well, I'll have to introduce you and then you'll see what I'm talking about. Lucas isn't so bad, but Mac makes me look laid back."

"Oh, my..."

"Exactly."

They stayed like that in companionable silence for several minutes before Maggie spoke again. "Hey, Jace?"

"Hmm?"

"Do you plan on going home tonight?"

"I hadn't planned on it. Why?"

If anything, she snuggled closer. "Just making sure we make the most of this before we return to the real world on Monday."

It was said innocently enough, but Jason had a feeling it was more like an ominous warning of things to come.

ELEVEN

SIX WEEKS after Jason and Maggie had returned from their trip, their work was done. Not completely done, because these were new clients and they'd be working with them for a long time, but all the initial setup and meetings were finally in place. It was a late Friday night and Jason was sitting at his desk staring at his computer screen, barely able to hold his head up, when his father walked in.

"Another late night?" William asked.

Jason nodded. "Hopefully the last one."

His father arched an eyebrow at him. "Seriously?"

Looking away from the computer, Jason focused on his father. "Yeah, seriously, why?"

"I'm just surprised to hear you talk like that. You are the king of the late-night negotiations. I thought you were going to move in here at one point."

"Ha ha, very funny," Jason said and then scrubbed a hand across his weary face.

"What's going on, Jace?"

What could he say? For weeks, Jason had felt a level of discontentment with his life. The long hours, going home alone, it was starting to wear on him. All of those feelings were compounded because he had little to no time to spend with Maggie. She was always patient and understanding, and they saw each other every day here in the office, but Jason knew it was just a matter of time before she'd had enough.

When they had been on the phone the previous night, Maggie had made a small comment about how there was a new movie out that she wanted to see on opening night. Tonight. Jason had told her he would try his best to leave the office early, and Maggie had just given him a sad laugh. When he pushed her for what was wrong, she'd told him she was just going to plan on going alone or with a friend.

The thought of her going out without him wasn't really an issue; the thought of her going out without him and meeting someone else did. Maggie was a beautiful woman, and since they had gotten back from Miami, she had blossomed with a new level of confidence. How long would it be before other men noticed that about her?

He'd tried feebly to explain his position and how important Montgomery's was to him. Her simple response of "But at what cost?" had hit him square in the chest. At what cost, indeed? Life was passing him by, and while everything he was doing was helping the company grow, Jason realized he'd lost friendships and missed out on weddings and parties and casual get-togethers with people who really mattered to him because he was spending his life behind a desk.

How much more was he willing to sacrifice for the sake of the company?

"Jace?" his father interrupted his thoughts.

"What? Sorry, Dad. I just sort of zoned out there for a minute."

"I thought you'd be with Maggie tonight." Jason's look of shock made his father laugh. "Oh, please, you didn't think you were going to hide that from me, did you?"

"We thought we were being careful," he grimaced.

"You were. I just knew what I was looking for."

"What the hell does that mean?"

William stood and waved his son off. "Nothing, nothing at all. Go home, Jace. Or go to Maggie's. Just leave the damn building and go and enjoy yourself for the weekend, for crying out loud. Montgomery's is not going to crumble and fall because you're not behind your desk."

Jason knew his father was right, and hated that he was that transparent. He stood and closed his laptop and packed up while William watched, and the two men left the office together. Placing an arm around his son's shoulder, William gave him a firm hug. "Life is meant to be enjoyed. There's nothing wrong with working hard, but you have to remember to focus on the people who mean the most to you."

"I do, Dad. I enjoy working with you and Mac and Lucas..."

"And Maggie?"

For a minute, Jason was sure he blushed. "And Maggie."

William's smile went from ear to ear. "You won't find a better woman than Maggie, Jace. Don't keep her waiting too long or some other lucky man will come in and sweep her off of her feet."

A frown marred Jason's features. Like hell some other man was going to take Maggie from him! "I have to go, Dad," Jason said, his stride quickening. He looked down at his watch and saw it was after ten. He had no idea if Maggie was home or at the movies, but no matter where she was, he would find her and maybe whisk her away for the weekend or bring her home to his place and pamper her. It didn't matter what they did, as long as he was with her.

In the time they'd been together, neither had made any grand commitments or even talked about their feelings. Well, that was going to end tonight. When he finally found her, Jason was going to tell her how he felt.

He just hoped he wasn't too late.

~

Tired of sitting home and waiting for the phone to ring, Maggie had taken a bold step and called an old friend to go to the movies with her. It had been a long time since she'd had a girls' night out and once she had parked her car at the theater and met up with her friend Theresa, she knew it was the right thing to do.

She had been too focused on Jason for weeks now, and found herself becoming more and more dissatisfied with the relationship. While she admired Jason's work ethic, it was becoming painfully obvious that work was Jason's first love and probably always would be. The thought made her sad because when he stepped away from the office, they always had an amazing time.

It wasn't all about sex, although that was fantastic. There were times they would stay up all night just talking, and Maggie loved hearing about all the places Jason had visited and what it was like growing up with his brothers. The problem was that as much as she loved spending time with him, she didn't see their relationship going anywhere, and she was tired of taking second place to Montgomery's.

After the movie, she and Theresa went out for coffee and dessert and spent the night just getting caught up with one another. It was well after midnight when she got home and while she was getting settled in, she remembered that she'd turned her cell phone off. Taking it from her purse, she turned it on and saw that she had several missed calls.

Eight of them, to be exact.

Sighing, she knew that each and every one of those missed calls was from Jason, and while she hadn't intentionally blown him off, she kind of felt that it served him right. See how he liked waiting all night for the phone to ring!

She was beyond tired after a long day at work and a late night out, but decided she should call him back. Changing into a pair of cotton boxers and a cami, she settled on the couch and dialed Jason's number.

"Maggie? Are you all right? Where have you been?" No greeting, just an anxious demand for answers.

"I'm fine, Jace, how are you?" she said, dripping sarcasm.

She heard his frustrated sigh. "Okay," he began. "I'm sorry. I was just worried about you. Your phone was off and I didn't know where you were!"

"I told you I wanted to go to the movies tonight. So I did."

"Alone?"

She didn't like his tone. Sure, they were sleeping together, but that didn't mean that she had to report to him every time she went out. "As a matter of fact, no." She knew she'd have to elaborate, but enjoyed his shocked silence. "I went with someone."

Jealousy obviously wasn't new to Jason, and there wasn't a doubt in her mind that he didn't like it. But he did his best to stay calm, but his words came out through clenched teeth. "With who?" he practically growled.

She could just picture the look on his face and almost burst out laughing. She knew that would only fuel his anger, but again, it served him right. "Actually, I met up with an old friend."

"Maggie," he said in his best menacing tone, letting her know she was testing his patience.

"I hadn't seen Theresa in well over a year. We met up at the theater, saw the movie, and then went out for coffee and dessert. It was a lovely night."

He let out a sigh of relief. "Oh... that's good. How was the movie?"

"We enjoyed it very much."

Unlike this conversation, which she wasn't.

As much as she wanted to talk to him, she was hurt. And tired. He needed to understand that she wasn't the type of woman who would be happy just to sit around and wait until he made time for her.

Maybe it was time for her to let him know.

"Look, Jace, it's late and I'm tired. I just wanted to call and let you know I was okay."

It was her tone. Jason knew Maggie well enough by now to know that something was definitely wrong. "I was worried about you," he said softly, "and I miss you."

She smiled sadly. "I miss you too. The thing is," she paused to collect her thoughts, "I can't keep doing this."

There, she'd said it.

"What do you mean?" Worry laced his voice and Jason had a feeling that he wasn't going to like the answer.

"I love being with you, but your work is your life, and I'm just starting to live mine again. I don't want to sit home waiting for the phone to ring or have you call me after you've already missed our date."

"That happened once—" he began, but she cut him off.

"It's been more than once, Jace, and you know it. I'm

not going to make you choose between Montgomery's and me. I think I need to step aside so I'm not a distraction."

Jason desperately wanted to get in the car and see her in person, to make her see how wrong she was. "You're not a distraction, dammit! You have to believe me! I know things have been crazy at work and I promise it's going to cut back some now. Things on the expansion are all in place; there won't be any more late nights, Maggie. Trust me. Please."

She wanted to believe him. Oh, how desperately she wanted to trust in him. "I think maybe we just need to take a break," she said quietly. "On Monday, I'll talk to Ann about finding you another assistant and..."

"Don't do this, Maggie," he said urgently. "I'm asking you not to do anything drastic. Give me a chance to prove to you that I can put work aside and put you first!"

A lone tear rolled down her cheek and she was glad she was all alone. "I don't want you to have to prove anything to me. I want to be important enough to someone that I'm a priority just because of who I am, not because I've laid a guilt trip or given an ultimatum. Eventually, you'll resent me for it, and you'll be making excuses to me or your family, and I just don't want to be in that position. I'm sorry."

"One more chance," he begged, his voice thick with emotion. "I'm not perfect, Maggie, I know that. All I'm asking is for you to let me make this right. I had no idea you were so unhappy. How can I possibly know if you don't tell me? And then how can I fix it if you won't let me?"

He had a point. Her mind was spinning and all she really wanted was to crawl into bed and sleep for a week. "Okay, Jason."

"Thank you, sweetheart. You won't regret it, I promise. No more missing dates, no more late nights at work. From here on out, I want you to know that you can count on me."

He paused and felt himself relax for the first time in hours. "Can I see you tomorrow? Maybe we can go to lunch and then..."

"I really think I need the weekend just for me," she said hesitantly. "I need to have a little time to myself, even though you've let me have more time alone than I wanted. I need to think about all that we talked about tonight."

"I'm not going to lie and tell you I'm not disappointed, because I am," he said honestly. "I wanted to see you tonight. I stopped by your place and I waited for an hour just to see you."

"Please don't try to make me feel guilty."

"No, I'm sorry; that was wrong of me. I just want you to know, Maggie, that when I'm not with you, I truly miss you."

More tears fell and she almost caved. "I miss you when we're not together, too, Jason. But it's really for the best for us to just take the weekend to do our own thing." She paused and wiped at her wet face. "I'll see you Monday morning, okay?"

"Okay. Sleep well, sweetheart," he said sadly.

"You, too."

TWELVE

BY MONDAY, Maggie felt much more in control of her emotions. She was confident that she could work with Jason and yet hold herself back enough that she would not be tempted to jump when he was ready to spend some time with her.

Jason was the consummate professional all day. As much as it pained him, he kept his distance and treated Maggie professionally, much as he had on their business trip. It wasn't until five o'clock that he finally was ready for something more.

"Maggie, can I see you in my office for a minute?" he asked as he saw her gathering her things to leave for the day.

"Sure," she said, placing her purse and jacket back down and following Jason into his office. "Was there something else you needed?" she asked once they were alone.

He smiled at her. He was a respectable foot away from her, and yet his fingers itched to touch her. Holding himself in check, he replied, "I was hoping that I could take you to dinner tonight."

Without conscious thought, Maggie launched herself

into his arms and initiated the kiss she had been craving for days. Jason was on board immediately and he lifted her off the ground as he reached for his office door and closed it. "I swore I wasn't going to do this," she said between kisses.

Jason's hands were finally on her, and it pained him to release her just long enough to lock the door. "This whole day has been hell for me; the weekend seemed as if it would never end." His words were clipped as he dragged his mouth along her jaw, down her neck, and then finally up to her lips again. His tongue dueled with hers and when he placed her back on her feet, he led her over to the large leather sofa and tugged her down with him.

She kicked off her shoes and smiled as Jason lay her down and lined his muscled body down on top of hers. He stroked her cheek and gazed down into her eyes. "You are so beautiful, Maggie," he said reverently. "I don't know what I ever did to deserve someone as beautiful as you."

She blushed at his words. A sassy comeback was on the tip of her tongue, but the way he was looking at her, she knew he was being deadly serious. She whispered, "thank you" and reached up to touch his face. His jaw was scratchy and it felt good against the palm of her hand.

"I love to look at you," he said, "to touch you." He paused as his hand wandered over her in the gentlest of caresses. "I love being with you."

"I love that, too," she replied. And in that moment, she realized something that made her heart actually lurch: she loved *him*. She was in love with Jason Montgomery.

Maggie wasn't sure when it actually happened. For all her issues with him as of late, the truth of the matter was she was so hurt because she was in love with him. She wanted to say the words to him, to tell him exactly how she felt, but he was lowering his head, his lips a whisper away from her own.

"I know I said dinner," he said softly, his breath hot against her mouth. "But I think I'd like to start with dessert."

"That's the best part," she said as she threaded her hands through his hair and pulled him down for what promised to be the most decadent of desserts.

They managed to make it out of the office and to dinner. Maggie was a little self-conscious of her slightly disheveled appearance, but the fact that she and Jason were finally out and away from the office made her slight discomfort worth it.

"I meant what I said, Maggie," he began as he reached across the table and took one of her hands in his. "I want a chance to prove to you that you're more important to me than work."

She smiled at him, but it didn't quite meet her eyes. "Jason, I don't expect you to change who you are. I fell in love with the man that you are." The words came out before she could stop them and by the look of surprise on Jason's face, she knew it was too late to take them back. That didn't stop her from trying, though. "What I mean is... I respect your work ethic and..."

"I'm in love with you, too," he interrupted.

There was so much she wanted to say, but their waiter appeared to take their orders. She was so flustered she could barely read the words on the menu through the tears of joy welling up in her eyes. "You order for us," she simply said to Jason and then delicately wiped at the tears threatening to fall.

When they were alone again, he leaned across the table and caressed her cheek. "I want a future with you, Maggie. I wasn't sure how you felt about me, especially after our conversation Friday night. I promise you, things are going to be different from here on out."

His words thrilled her and if there was one thing she knew about Jason, he did his best to be a man of his word. She knew she could trust him and that their issues with the relationship could probably just be attributed to poor timing. After all, Montgomery's was in a time of major transition, and she would be foolish to think something of that magnitude wasn't going to impact Jason's life.

"I want us to go back to New York," he began. "I want us to take a real vacation where we can relax. I was thinking maybe a long weekend at the Four Seasons. What do you think?"

She remembered the amazing room and the spa bathroom and how she had fantasized about sharing it all with him. "I think that sounds perfect! Let's do it!"

Jason found himself thrilled that they were on the same page, and he could finally see a future for himself beyond working late nights and going home alone. If anyone had told him six months ago that he'd fall in love with his assistant, he would have told them they were crazy. As much as he hated the comparison, knowing how Lucas and Emma had made it work, he was confident he and Maggie had just as big a future ahead of them. Nothing and no one was going to get in his way.

A week and a half later, Jason was sitting at his desk smiling. Reservations were made for their weekend away, and Jason had planned the most romantic getaway ever. They would leave right from work on Friday, take the private plane up to New York, where a limo would take them to the Four Seasons. He had dinner reservations right in the hotel because he knew that once they got there, it would be late, and he wanted to make the most of their time in the room.

On Saturday, they would go out and explore and shop. He made plans to take that carriage ride through Central Park, where he was going to ask Maggie to marry him. He thought he might be moving too fast, but now that he knew what he wanted for his future, he was eager to put it in motion.

Mac walked in and rolled his eyes at the sappy look on Jason's face. "All right, we get it, you're in love," he said dramatically before sitting down in a chair facing his brother. "Geez, I don't know who is more sickening, you or Lucas!"

"Please, you're just jealous. And Lucas hasn't been sickening for a while," Jason replied, keeping his tone light. Nothing was going to bring him down, not when his future with Maggie was right within his reach.

"You mean he hasn't been in here yet?" Mac asked.

"I didn't even know Lucas was in the office today. What's going on?"

Mac waved him off. "I'll let him tell you."

As if on cue, Lucas walked in and Mac was right, his sappy grin was worse than Jason's. "Emma's pregnant," he said as he came to a stop in Jason's office. Jason stood and came around to hug his brother.

"That is great news! How is she feeling?"

"So far, so good. We realize that could all change at any time and morning sickness could set in, but for right now, everything is great."

The brothers stood and laughed and did their best to rib Lucas on how much his life was going to change, but Jason's words were halfhearted at best. "What's going on with you?" Lucas finally asked, suspicious of his brother's lack of sarcasm at his expense.

"I'm going to ask Maggie to marry me," he said, his chest puffed out with pride.

"Oh, for crying out loud," Mac grumbled. "Already?"

Lucas punched Mac in the arm. "I cannot wait for it to be your turn, Mac. You are going to fall harder than the rest of us and you can be sure we'll be right there, sitting on the sidelines, mocking you!"

"Do it and die." Mac glared.

"Wait and see..." Lucas said before turning back to Jason. "So, when are you doing it?"

Jason told them both of his plans for the upcoming weekend and Lucas wished him luck. "Listen, I'd love to stay and talk some more, but we're having dinner with Mom and Dad and I have to go and pick up Emma. Good luck, bro!"

Once he was gone and it was just Jason and Mac, Mac turned and closed the door and got serious.

"What's going on?" Jason asked, concern lacing his tone.

"We were contacted by a major company who wants to do business with us," he began cautiously. "If it all goes as I can see it going, this one company has the potential to bring in more business than all the companies you just signed on."

Jason collapsed into his seat. "Damn, that's huge! Who are they? When do they want to meet?"

Mac stared down at him and watched as the realization hit Jason. "I'm not going to like this, am I?" Jason asked.

"Brother, you don't know the half of it."

~

Maggie was giddy for their weekend. She took off early on Friday so she could go home and pack. Jason was going to pick her up at six and their flight was at seven. Ever since they had admitted their feelings to one another, Maggie had been floating on a cloud. She was afraid to let herself hope too much, but she had a feeling Jason might propose this weekend.

He had done nothing outright to give her that impression, but they were so in tune with one another that she just had a feeling. She wouldn't be disappointed if he didn't, but she couldn't help but wonder how he would actually do it. Would he be traditional and get down on one knee? Would it be someplace public? Would they be alone? Her heart raced at all of those scenarios because, at the end of it all, she really wanted to be Mrs. Jason Montgomery.

Jason had been true to his word and had cut back on the late nights at the office. They had been spending more time together and he had actually asked Maggie to move in with him. She had planned on giving him her answer this weekend and that answer was going to be yes! As much as she loved having her own place, the hassle of going between their homes and packing stuff for overnights was just getting to be a pain. Plus, she wanted to wake up with the man she loved every morning and not have to think about where they were going to be the next night.

She was throwing the last of her cosmetics into her luggage when she realized she had left her phone charger back at the office. While it would be easy to call Jason and just have him bring it, she knew he had enough on his plate today. Looking at her watch, she saw it was only two o'clock. The office was only ten minutes away and there were a few last-minute errands she needed to run; one more stop would not make a difference.

The drive over to the office was quick and when Rose saw her, she faltered in her steps. "Maggie? We didn't expect you back this afternoon."

"Just forgot my phone charger," she replied, smiling as she held it up. "What's going on?"

"Oh, nothing," Rose said, looking over her shoulder. "They've got a client in there and I need to get back. I hope you have a good weekend." And then she was gone.

"Well, that was odd," Maggie said under her breath and then looked toward Jason's office. His door was open but the lights were off, so she figured he was in with either Mac or his father. Walking toward Mac's office, she noticed his was also dark, so she stopped at his assistant's empty desk. That was odd, too. Maggie didn't remember them having any appointments on the calendar, and Diana rarely left her desk.

Looking around, Maggie took a glance at the open planner on her coworker's desk and gasped. "No," she whispered. Walking briskly, she headed toward William Montgomery's suite. When she approached Rose's desk, she stopped short. "Is Jason in there?" she asked sharply.

Rose couldn't quite meet her eyes. "Maggie, don't worry about what's going on in there. You're supposed to be getting ready for your weekend."

Maggie arched her brows at Rose. How much did the other woman know about her relationship with Jason? They hadn't been particularly secretive these last weeks, but it still irked her a little to know that everyone was privy to their business. "I am more than ready for my weekend. Why wasn't I informed about this meeting?"

Rose sighed. "It was a last-minute thing and really, it's nothing you need to worry about."

"Why don't you let me be the judge of that?" Her voice came out louder than she had planned and suddenly Jason was stepping out of his father's office.

"Maggie? What are you doing here? I thought you left early to go home and pack?"

"Why is everyone so concerned about my packing?" she asked. "I'm already packed and I forgot my phone charger here. I had some errands to run and thought I'd swing by and get it. I didn't realize I wasn't allowed to come to my place of business. Care to tell me why that is?" She glared at him while waiting for an answer.

"No one said you weren't allowed here, Maggie, it was just that we all thought..."

"What? You thought that you could plan a business meeting with the one person who you know I would have a problem with? I cannot believe you, Jason! When is it ever going to be enough? You have more business than you can handle and you know my history with this particular client, and yet you still invited him here to do business?" Her eyes welled with tears, and she cursed herself for showing weakness.

Part of her knew she shouldn't be surprised. Montgomery's was always going to come first, but she didn't think it would hurt so much or that Jason and William would choose to do business with Martin Blake. Her heart actually hurt, and when Jason went to reach for her hand, she jerked away from him.

"You know, there are a lot of things I can overlook. I understand your commitment to your family and to your business, but I can't work for someone or live with someone that I don't trust. You knew my feelings about this and rather than talk to me, you snuck behind my back to meet with him."

"Maggie," Jason began, but she cut him off.

"No, I'm done, Jason. You asked me for a second chance and I gave it. You asked me to trust you, and I did. But this?" She waved toward the office. "This is something I can't overlook. I don't doubt for a second that Martin made some outrageous offer to you, and I can't blame you for wanting the business. It's just not something I want any part of."

"You don't understand," Jason pleaded. "Let's go to my office and I'll—"

"Hey, Mags," Martin Blake said as he strolled into the outer office. "Fancy seeing you here." His gaze raked over her and Maggie felt violated all over again. "I had to do a little research to see who the big shot you were working for was, and after talking to Alan down in Miami, he told me all about Montgomerys. I figured, if Alan's working with them, then we should, too. It'll be like old times, right, Mags?"

She wanted to vomit. Her lunch turned in her stomach, and she couldn't believe Jason just stood there and let Martin even talk to her. She was just about to comment on it when Martin asked Rose where the men's room was. Once he was out of earshot, she glared at Jason.

"Let's go talk," Jason said again.

"No," she said adamantly. "I'm done talking. I quit." She turned and walked away, her stride quickening to get to the elevator. She expected Jason to come after her, or at least to call her name. But he didn't. When the elevator arrived in the lobby, she expected him to come out through the door to the stairway to stop her. But he didn't.

How could she have been so wrong about him? How could she have misunderstood all the plans they had been making? By the time she reached her car, Maggie could barely see through the haze of tears. She had trusted Jason; she had put her trust *in* Jason, and he had betrayed her, all in the name of business.

She felt numb and hollow and didn't know where to go or what to do. The thought of going home was unappealing because all her luggage was packed, full of promises for a romantic weekend that was never going to happen. She was now without a job and had no idea where her life was going to go from here. So, she put the car in gear and drove. She had no direction, so she just hit the interstate and let the miles fill the void inside of her.

Jason was frantic. He wanted to run after Maggie and explain everything, but he knew her mind was made up and there was nothing he was going to be able to say to make her see things for the way they really were.

Not that he could blame her; if he were in her shoes, he wouldn't believe him either.

"Why didn't you go after her?" his father said quietly behind him.

"She wasn't going to listen."

"You don't know that, Jace. She didn't know what was going on."

"I know Maggie. I've screwed up too much, and no matter what I said, she wasn't going to believe me."

"I told you, you should have been up front with her. No good ever comes from lying, Son."

Jason turned and looked at his father. "What was I supposed to do? Admit that this slimy piece of crap contacted us and the only way I could ensure he never, ever got near her again was to bring him here and confront him?

Threaten him with financial ruin if he ever did to another woman what he did to Maggie? She wouldn't agree with it!"

"All I'm saying is..."

"And then he came out here and started talking like we were honestly going to do business together! There was no way for me to tell her the truth with him blathering on like an idiot."

"You should have gone after her and made her listen," his father said patiently.

"To what end, Dad? She's never going to trust me again and I can't blame her. She was finally moving on with her life and the only times she's had to face that bastard was because of me! The hurt in her eyes..." he said and his voice clogged with emotion. "I'll never be able to forgive myself for being the one to put that look there."

Just then, Martin walked out of the restroom and looked from William to Jason. "Ready to sign?" he asked, walking back into William's office with a confident swagger.

Jason glared at the man and then looked at his father. "Let's finish this."

THIRTEEN

MAGGIE DROVE for hours and eventually ended up back at her apartment.

And that just made her sad that she literally had nowhere else to go.

She half expected to find Jason there, but he wasn't.

Sluggishly, she walked up to her door and let herself in. The silence was deafening. It was a little after eight and she sighed sadly at how they would have been landing in New York now and on their way to the hotel. She would never know what Jason had planned for the weekend; it would always be a "what if" scenario in her mind.

Her body was weak and her mind was blank as she went about unpacking her luggage and carefully putting things away. She looked at the sexy negligee she had bought at Victoria's Secret and wanted to burn it. She'd never get to wear it; even if she lived to be one hundred and had dozens of lovers, she would never allow herself to wear it because she had bought it with Jason in mind.

But she was nothing if not practical, and so she kept it

securely wrapped in tissue and tucked into the back of her drawer.

Out of sight, out of mind.

When the last of her stuff was put away, she decided to order dinner. Collapsing on the sofa, she scrolled through her phone to the food deliver app and tried to figure out what she wanted. She had no appetite, but knew she needed to eat. No sense in making herself sick on top of having a broken heart. With her Chinese food ordered, she changed into a pair of yoga pants and an oversized T-shirt and flipped on the TV to distract her until it arrived.

Thirty minutes later, there was a knock on the door, and she padded over to answer it. William Montgomery stood on the threshold with her takeout bag in his hand. "Mr. Montgomery? What are you doing here?"

"May I come in?" he asked quietly.

As much as she would have loved to slam the door in his face, after all, he was involved in that whole debacle earlier too, she just didn't have the heart to do it. Instead, she nodded and stepped aside.

"I hope you don't mind that I swooped in and shang-haied your delivery boy." He took a whiff and smiled. "Is that Szechuan I smell?"

"It's fine," she said shyly, "and yes." Taking the bag from his hands, she walked to the kitchen to place it down. Now her appetite was completely gone. What in the world was she supposed to say to this man? Not only was he her boss... er, former boss, but he was the father of the man who had just destroyed her life. "Can I get you something to drink?" she asked, trying to keep her voice calm and steady.

"No. I'm fine. May I sit?"

Maggie inclined her head toward the living room and

waited for him to take a seat on her sofa before sitting across from him on the matching love seat. "What can I do for you?" she asked carefully.

"Well, that was going to be my line," he said with a soft chuckle. "I wanted to make sure you were alright."

She smiled sadly at him. "I'm not okay, but I will be. Eventually."

William leaned forward, his elbows on his knees. "Maggie, I know that things looked bad this afternoon…"

"Please don't," she interrupted. "I just need this whole ugly phase of my life to be over. Martin Blake was the reason I came to Montgomerys and I guess it's only fitting that he is the reason I'm leaving. I'll admit I was shocked by his appearance there today, but I understand that business is business. It was stupid of me to expect you to lose a big client just because of something that happened to me years ago."

"Maggie, look at me," William said softly, and he didn't say another word until she did. "I didn't tell Jason or anyone that I was coming here. I wanted you to know there was never going to be a business deal with Martin Blake. He approached us with a very attractive offer, and had it come from anyone else, we would have jumped at the opportunity. Knowing what we do, however, that was never going to happen."

Maggie looked confused. "Then why was he there? Why was it such a big secret?"

William sighed wearily. "Jason wanted to protect you. Martin was aggressive in his approach and wasn't willing to take no for an answer over the phone, so Mac and Jason thought it best to take the meeting with him and take care of it in person."

"But when Martin came out of your office, he said we'd be working together! That he was looking forward to doing business..."

"I'll admit we strung him along a little," he replied sheepishly. "It made it just that much more fun to let him down."

Confusion was written all over Maggie's face. "I'm not following you..."

William stood and then sat beside Maggie on the love seat. "Maggie, Jason wanted to confront Martin face to face. He and Mac had done a little investigating and found out that you weren't the only woman Martin had harassed. So, once we had him in the office, Jason confronted him with what he'd found and threatened to ruin him financially if he ever came near you or any other woman like that again. You never have to worry about the likes of Martin Blake bothering you ever again."

"But... how...?"

"Of course, he was defiant at first; a little combative, even." He shrugged. "Then he begged and groveled for a bit before practically daring us to do something." He shook his head. "Such an arrogant little punk. So, for a little extra fun, I forwarded the report our private investigator found to all of Martin's business associates." He gave her a lopsided grin. "Technically, we kept our word; he simply pushed our hand."

"So, you were never...?"

"Never, Maggie. You have to believe me. There was never going to be a deal where we'd work with someone like him. Family means more than that."

"But... I'm not family," she said weakly.

This time his smile was sad. "No. Not yet. But I was hopeful."

That's when it hit her. "Oh my God," she whispered. "What have I done?"

William reached for her hand and gave her a comforting squeeze. "You did what anyone would do in your position. I had hoped that Jason would tell you what was going on, but he thought it was best to keep it a secret until it was over. He didn't want you worrying or being uncomfortable. Mostly, he didn't want you to worry about seeing Martin. He thought he was doing what was right."

Tears streamed down her face. "And I accused him of being selfish when he was trying to protect me. What am I supposed to do now?" Maggie stood and began pacing her small living room.

"Go to him, Maggie. He's at home kicking himself for what he put you through."

Without conscious thought, Maggie grabbed her purse and keys, threw on a pair of sneakers, and was about to run out the door before she remembered that William was still standing in her living room. "Help yourself to some Chinese, but I have to go!" Slamming the door behind her, Maggie rushed down to her car and hoped that on the drive to Jason's, she'd figure out just what exactly she was going to say.

All wasn't completely forgiven, the man was going to have to learn to actually communicate with her and not simply take matters into his own hands.

Especially when said matters pertained directly to her.

"Yeah. We're going to talk about that."

And they were going to talk about how Maggie wasn't some damsel in distress anymore. She could take care of herself and he needed to let her do that. As much as she appreciated the fact that he wanted to fight her battles and take care of her, he needed to trust that there were going to be times when she could do that for herself.

There wasn't a doubt in her mind that they were going to get through this, but she wanted him to see her as an equal; a partner.

She was due her happily ever after, dammit.

And she wanted it with this man.

This infuriatingly stubborn, clueless man who was too noble for his own good sometimes.

He might be used to being the one to take of everything and everybody, but this time, he was going to have to sit back and be prepared for someone to take care of him.

And Maggie knew she was the perfect woman for the job.

$\sim$

It was a starless night.

Jason sat out on his deck, letting the early winter weather wrap around him. He could have grabbed a blanket, he could have put on a sweater, but he hadn't. He'd probably get pneumonia from it, but he didn't care. Nothing mattered anymore, not without Maggie.

Why hadn't he listened to his father and just told her what was going on? Why had he been so insistent that it all be a secret? His father had never steered him wrong, and the one time he went against his father's advice, it had cost him everything.

He took a pull from the beer he was drinking and it tasted bitter going down. Right now, he should have been drinking champagne in the penthouse suite and eating chocolate off of Maggie's body. They would have been enjoying the sight of the New York skyline and making love and planning their future. He reached into his pocket and played with the ring meant to go on her finger, but now never would.

Now he was just sitting alone outside in the cold kicking himself.

Some Friday night.

All night he'd been cursing himself. Why didn't he try harder to make her listen? Why hadn't he gone after her? Why had he just admitted defeat?

Because you'd let her down so many times already...

Oh, yeah. That.

Staring up at the sky, he wondered where she was. Did she go home? Did she go to a friend's house? He hoped she wasn't sitting home alone like he was. This was its own form of hell. There was no one to talk to, and even the voices in his head were against him.

And it was no more than he deserved.

A loud pounding on his front door shook him out of his reverie. He placed his beer down on the deck and walked into the house. His hair was disheveled and his shirt was open, his feet bare. Jason had no idea who could be at his door at this hour, but he didn't give a damn about how he looked.

It was probably one of his brothers, or maybe his father coming to check on him. He'd let them in, but he really didn't want to see or talk to anyone. They'd probably take one look at him and realize just how miserable he was. He was the kind of man who always looked put together even when he was home alone or casually hanging out with friends.

"They're your family, dumbass. They've seen you looking less than perfect," he murmured.

But when he opened the door, he wished he had taken the time to put himself mildly back together.

"Maggie?" he asked in disbelief. "What are you doing here?"

She didn't answer right away; she was too taken aback by Jason's appearance. She had seen Jason dressed in suits and tuxedos and in jeans and T-shirts. She'd seen him first thing in the morning all mussed up from sleep, and slick with sweat after making love, but she had never seen him look so utterly devastated. Holding her tongue, she stepped around him and into the foyer and waited for him to shut the door.

"You lied to me," she said by way of an opening.

He could only nod.

As much as he wanted to defend himself, he knew it had taken a lot of courage for her to come here and confront him, so he would not interrupt her. She deserved to have her say without him trying to make her see his point of view.

"Why didn't you tell me the real reason you had Martin at Montgomerys?" she demanded softly.

"I tried to tell you, Maggie, but you wouldn't..." He stopped. "I should have told you from the beginning. I'm sorry I didn't."

She nodded. "Yes, you should have." The look of defeat on Jason's face was almost more than she could bear. "I don't appreciate having you make decisions for me and thinking that you know what's best."

"That wasn't my intention. I swear. I honestly wanted to protect you from ever having to see him again. In Miami, you told me how it had taken you months to be able to close your eyes and not see him or hear him. I thought I was doing the right thing."

She was about to walk into the living room, but she stopped and turned to face him again. "That was *before*, Jason! I don't have to be afraid of him anymore, and do you know why?"

He shook his head.

"It's because of you! I know that there is nothing someone like Martin Blake can do to me, and even back then, I did nothing wrong. I don't have to hide. I don't have to feel ashamed. I would have *loved* the opportunity to see his face when you told him you had proof of all the hideous things he's done!"

Jason's eyes went wide. "I didn't want him anywhere near you!" He strode toward her and grabbed her by the shoulders. "I never want anyone ever to hurt you again, Maggie. Don't you understand?"

She looked up at him and saw in his eyes how much he meant what he was saying. "But you hurt me, Jace. You didn't trust me enough."

"Sweetheart, I do trust you. I honestly thought I was doing the right thing. I wanted to make it all go away and know he couldn't ever hurt you again."

"He couldn't, Jason. He doesn't hold that power over me anymore, and I have you to thank for that. You did that for me back in Miami. I'm stronger now. You make me stronger! I wanted us to be strong together."

He pulled her closer and was relieved when she didn't pull away. "We are stronger together. When you walked out today, I thought I'd lost everything. Please tell me we're okay. Tell me you're here because you know I love you and I need you."

No words came to mind because she was so overwhelmed with emotion. So she answered him the only way she knew how. Stepping up and aligning their bodies, Maggie reached up and threaded her fingers through his mussed hair, and pulled him down for a scorching kiss. She felt his sigh of relief as he pulled her tight against him. When they finally broke apart, Maggie cupped his face and stared up at the man that she loved. "I'm here because I love and need you, too."

"Thank God," he said before reclaiming her mouth with his.

~

Hours later, sprawled out in Jason's bed, Maggie let out a very contented sigh.

"We should have hopped on a plane," Jason said as his fingers gently caressed her back.

"It would have been too much running around and stressful."

"Yeah, but we'd be having strawberries and champagne while looking up at the stars and enjoying room service."

"Highly over-rated."

"Maggie..."

Lifting her head, she met his gaze. "Okay, I'm only going to say this one more time and then we will never have this discussion again."

"Um..."

"I'm not with you for the luxury trips and the expensive hotels and all the perks that go with dating a Montgomery. I'm with you because I genuinely like you as a person. You're sweet and kind and funny; you make me laugh, you make me think, and you make me crazy," she added with a sassy wink. "I look at you and my heart races and flutters.

You're far too sexy for your own good and when you kiss me, I forget my own name."

If she wasn't mistaken, he was actually blushing.

Or preening.

The lighting was dim and she couldn't be sure.

"Either way, I don't care if we never leave the state of North Carolina. I love being with you just for you. The trips and the hotels are nice, but... they're not a necessity. I loved going to New York with you and I was looking forward to experiencing it as a couple, but... the city isn't going anywhere. There will be other times. Tonight, we needed to be here and make things right between us."

He let out a long sigh. "I know, but..."

"No," she interrupted. "That's all there is to it. There is nothing up there that is more important that what we can do here."

"Well...I wouldn't exactly say that..."

That piqued her curiosity. "Oh?"

"Let's just say that...I had everything planned out and there was something...special that I specifically wanted to do," he said miserably.

Sitting up a little more, Maggie studied him. "And you can't do it here?"

"Um..."

"Was it food?"

"No."

"Was it a show? Because you know a lot of them travel and maybe we can see it here sometime."

"It wasn't a show."

"Hmm... was it a hockey game?" She gasped. "Oh, my goodness. It was a hockey game, wasn't it?" Pausing, she thought for a moment. "Dammit, and they're playing

Tampa Bay this weekend. Ugh! That would have been a great game!"

He sighed again. "It wasn't a hockey game."

Now she was confused. "So, it wasn't food, a show, or a game. I know we talked about some of the sites we were going to see, but nothing that should have you this freaked out."

"I'm not freaked out," he argued weakly, but he was definitely pouting.

"Jason, come on. Talk to me."

Rather than respond, he rolled away from her and then got up and walked out of the room.

Dumbfounded, she could only stare after him. "Well, that was a little rude..."

Five minutes later, he strode back in, still naked, but carrying a bottle of champagne and two glasses.

"Just for the record, I'm impressed with how you are so comfortable that you walked around your entire house naked," she told him with a grin. "I would have totally needed a robe before I even left the room."

"Yeah, I'm not as brave as I look," he said with a small laugh. "I felt wildly uncomfortable the entire time, but... it was necessary."

Eyeing the champagne, she wouldn't have called it a necessity, but clearly, he did.

Placing the glasses on the bedside table, Jason took a moment to open the champagne and poured them each a glass. The cork fell on the floor and she watched with amusement as he crouched down to find it.

When he didn't stand right back up, she went to lean over the mattress. "Did it roll under the bed or something?"

"What? Um... no. Here it is," he murmured, his back to her.

Picking up one of the glasses, Maggie moved back over to her side of the bed and got comfortable propped up against the pillows and pulled the sheet up a bit to cover herself because...modesty.

When Jason joined her back on the bed, he had his champagne in his hand and looked wildly uncomfortable.

"Jace? You okay?"

He nodded, but didn't say anything for a few moments.

"Maggie," he began. "I'm so sorry for the way things went today. I had this perfect weekend planned for us..."

"Jason, I told you..."

But he held up a hand to stop her.

"I had this perfect weekend planned for us, and I kind of hate that we're sitting here rather than in our suite at the Four Seasons." Pausing, he shifted slightly. "I love you and all I want is to give you the life that you deserve. I know you say it's not important, but I do want to travel with you and share some of the experiences that I think we'd both enjoy. I want to spend every day having the greatest adventures of our lives together."

Her heart melted a little.

"But more than anything, I want to spend every day showing you just how much you are loved." That's when he reached out and took one of her hands in his. "I fought having an assistant and I remember after meeting you for the first time how I thought you were so wrong for me." He grinned. "But I've never been so happy to be proven wrong. You were the perfect woman for me and not just as an assistant, but as a friend, a lover, and, if you'll have me, as a wife."

She gasped softly as Jason released her hand and reached behind him.

Then he held up a ring.

"Maggie Barrett, I love you. I'm always going to love you. And I promise right now that I will always come to you with what I'm thinking and planning and never take you for granted ever again. Will you marry me?"

With tears stinging her eyes, she nodded. "Yes," she whispered. "There is nothing in the world that I want more. I love you."

And they sealed it with a kiss.

EPILOGUE

"YOU KNOW people think we're crazy, right?"

Maggie shrugged. "I don't care."

"We had at least fifty other options that would have been more fitting."

Glancing over her shoulder at him, she gave him a bland stare. "Still don't care."

Jason leaned back in his seat and huffed. "I can't believe we missed going to Paris for this."

Just then, Maggie jumped to her feet. "Oh, come on!" she yelled. "He hooked him! What is wrong with that ref?" Slumping back into her seat, she reached for her beer and pouted.

"Need I remind you that we could be drinking champagne at the Eiffel Tower right now," Jason said in a teasing tone, "rather than sitting here in this cold arena watching your team get slaughtered?"

Maggie turned and punched him in the arm. "They're not getting slaughtered, and you were the one who got the tickets for the playoffs," she reminded him.

"I didn't think you'd actually choose this over Paris for our honeymoon," he pouted.

"Aw..." She leaned in and kissed him sweetly. "I didn't choose this *over* Paris. I just chose to stop here first."

"All I'm saying is I want to take you on a romantic getaway and you keep thwarting all my best attempts." He wanted to say more, but his new bride was up on her feet again, cheering as the Rangers scored and tied up the game.

"When are you going to learn that it doesn't matter to me where we are, just as long as we're together?"

He stood, wrapped her in his arms, and pulled her in for another kiss. "I'm a slow learner where you're concerned," he admitted. "But I promise to get better."

"Excellent," she purred against his lips. "Besides, this little side trip makes up for the trip we missed when you proposed."

"Yeah, sorry it took so long to reschedule."

"Well, with you wanting me to move in right away and then all the wedding planning, there just wasn't time. I'm not complaining; this is perfect timing as far as I'm concerned."

They sat back down and Maggie rested her head on Jason's shoulder, sighing with happiness.

Yes, having the man she loved sitting beside her while watching the team she loved, knowing that their future was wide open ahead of them, was definitely worth the wait.

WHO WILL WILLIAM MONTGOMERY
MATCH UP NEXT??

Find out in

WITH ME

PROLOGUE

STANDING OUTSIDE on a crisp September morning, William Montgomery swore that the sun was shining directly on him. The morning dew sparkled on the lush acres of green grass before him as he awaited the arrival of his dearest friend to join him for a round of golf.

The last two years had left him feeling blessed; two of his three sons were married, he had a grandchild on the way, and he was about to spend some quality time outside with a friend on a beautiful day. Yes, William was most definitely a blessed man. Inhaling deeply, he lifted his face to the sun, smiled, and thanked the good Lord above.

"Now that is the face of a man at peace," a voice said from behind.

Turning, William greeted his lifelong friend Arthur Micelli and shook his hand. "That I am, Art, that I am. How could I not be?"

A sad smile crossed his friend's face. "As long as you appreciate it, Will. Embrace it."

Something in Arthur's tone caused a trickle of alarm. William wanted to come right out and ask if everything was all right but knew better than to charge into what could quite possibly be a delicate situation. So instead of asking what was on the tip of his tongue, he segued into the next order of business. "You ready for eighteen holes?"

Arthur looked out at the greens ahead of them and sighed. "No time like the present."

Something was definitely up. "I don't know about you, Art, but I don't feel much like walking this one. I'm going to grab a cart, and then we'll get started. What do you say?"

Arthur's shoulders sagged with what William would guess was relief. "Sounds good to me." Within minutes, their bags were loaded and they were on their way. At first, the conversation consisted of the basic pleasantries, but by the third hole, William was ready to get a little more insight into what was going on with his friend.

"You feeling okay, Art?"

His friend chuckled. "You know me too well." Climbing from the cart, he stood and waited for William to join him. They stood side by side for a long, quiet moment before Arthur spoke. "Remember when the kids were little and we'd all get together in the summertime to barbecue and go swimming?"

"Those are some of my fondest memories from when they were all growing up. Just listening to their laughter as they chased each other around always brought a smile to my face." William smiled even now at the thought of it. "Which reminds me, how is Gina doing? Have you talked to her lately?"

The mention of Arthur's daughter seemed to bring on a wave of sadness followed by regret. "We spoke on the phone briefly last week."

"How's she doing?"

"The same. Working for a firm she doesn't seem to like

very much and doing her best not to disappoint her mother."

"That's a shame. I really thought Barb would have outgrown that controlling streak of hers."

"I think it got worse after the divorce, and unfortunately, Gina's paying the price for it."

"She's a grown woman, Art; she can move away anytime she wants. California isn't the only place she can live. Hell, she can come back here to North Carolina! Have you approached her about coming to work for you?"

Arthur shook his head. "As much as I would love for Gina to move back here by me, I would never ask."

"Why not?" William asked, stunned. "I would do whatever it took to get my child back in my life."

"Don't you see, Will? She's never had the opportunity to choose to do anything. Barb has made all of her decisions for her. The poor girl has never been allowed to decide what it is *she* wants to do. If I call and ask her to come here and work with me, she'd probably say yes out of guilt and then stress herself out because she'd know that her mother would be angry with her." He sighed wearily. "I don't want to add any more stress to her life. Thanks to me, she's suffered enough."

"That's a bunch of bull and you know it!" William snapped. "Your wife chose to leave and took your daughter with her. If anything, you stepped back in hopes of making Gina's life easier. You're still stepping back!"

"It's hard, William; you don't understand. You and Monica have a great marriage and your sons are all with you. You're luckier than you realize. I envy you."

The sadness in Art's voice had William rethinking this line of conversation. "Well, that's kind of you to say, but it's not always smooth sailing. Hell, in the last couple of years, my sons have been more than a little irritated with me a time or two." He chuckled as he thought of how their irritation had faded when they'd realized that dear old dad was doing them the greatest favor of their lives by finding them the perfect wives. So far, Lucas and Jason were enjoying the very lives they had rebelled against, and nothing could please William more.

He just wished Arthur and his daughter could reconcile their differences.

"Remember when the kids were younger and we always thought it would be great if Gina married one of the boys?"

Art laughed. "We always thought she should marry Lucas because they were the closest in age, but she only had eyes for Mac."

William felt a familiar itch of inspiration. "She sure did, followed him around wherever he went. He may have grumbled about it at the time, but I think that was just to save face."

Arthur couldn't help but smile at the memory as well. "Well, seeing as he's seven years older than Gina, I'm sure it wasn't cool to have her trailing around after him." He turned toward William. "He was always a good sport about it. I was always so grateful that he made sure to be kind. No wonder she had such a crush on him!"

"Lucky for us he's the only one left who isn't married!"

"If only it were that simple," Art said. "They haven't seen each other in, what? Twelve or thirteen years?"

"What difference does that make?" William's voice boomed with excitement. "There's still time! I bet if we got them together, there'd still be a lingering spark. Plus, they're no longer kids. Just think, we could be grandparents together in no time!"

Art turned to his friend with a look of utter devastation.

William stopped and looked at Arthur's face, seeing the fatigue etched there and that his color was a little off.

"Art? What's going on?" A cool breeze blew around them and the sun dipped behind a cloud, as if sensing the impending news. His friend's hesitation stopped William cold. "Art?"

"I'm dying."

CHAPTER 1

MACKENZIE MONTGOMERY WAS TIRED.

Weary to the bone exhausted, really.

It wasn't the long hours at the office wearing him out; it was the incessant rounds of well-wishers with their "Congratulations" and "You all must be so happy" that were grating on his every last nerve.

"*Must* I be so happy?" he muttered under his breath.

Deep down, Mac knew they all meant well; he shouldn't begrudge their pleasantries. Unfortunately, for the last two years, all he'd seemed to hear was how happy everyone was for his brothers, their wives, their lives...Sure, it was great, but didn't anyone have anything else to think about? To focus on?

"Great news about Lucas and Emma, isn't it, Mac?"

Mac looked up, and there in the doorway stood one of his junior executives with an eager look and a wide smile on his young face. Mac tried to return the smile, but at this point in the day, it made his face hurt. "It sure is."

"Tell them I said congratulations!" the young man said before disappearing.

Mac slumped down into his plush leather chair and turned to face his wall of windows. The sun was starting to set and the view of downtown Charlotte was one of bustling activity. Glancing at his watch, he saw that it was just after five, and he knew he should head to the hospital where the rest of his family had congregated to welcome the newest Montgomery.

A girl. Mac couldn't help but chuckle. His former NFL player brother, who had been so certain he was going to have a son to teach all of his moves to, now had a tiny baby girl. There was a joke in there somewhere, but right now Mac couldn't seem to find it. He'd go, meet the newest member of the family, pat Lucas on the back and hug Emma, and remember to smile at all of the excitement that was sure to be going on around him. But all he really wanted to do was go home, have a beer, and just relax.

Alone.

The drive to the hospital was short, and he even remembered to stop and pick up a bouquet of flowers for his sister-in-law. As he headed toward Emma's room, the noise level told him his prediction was right on the money. He was greeted by his father first, then his brother Jason, finally making his way to shake the new father's hand before handing the flowers to Emma.

"Oh, Mac," Emma said as tears swam in her eyes. "They're perfect. Lilies for our Lily."

Right, the baby's name was Lily. Happy coincidence? Or maybe he had subconsciously remembered his father telling him that was what they had named her. Neither here nor there, the fact was he had done a good thing and now everyone was staring at him with sappy grins on their faces.

Great.

"Do you want to hold her?" Emma asked, nodding toward the bassinet next to her bed.

Mac was about to break out in a cold sweat. Hold her? *The baby?* Wasn't that against the rules or something? He wasn't the father! He could give her germs or drop her! Lucas must have seen the look of pure terror on his face because he chuckled and said, "I'm not ready to entrust my princess with him yet. He can't even catch a football!" The room erupted with laughter, but Mac took it all in stride since it got him out of infant holding.

"Were you planning on throwing her to me? Because I'm pretty sure the hospital has rules against that," he teased and then smiled when his mother came over and looped her arm though his, pulling him close.

"You'll have to hold her eventually," she whispered with a sassy smile.

"Sure, when she's talking in complete sentences, I'm sure I'll be fine."

He heard his father's cell phone ring in the distance and watched as William quickly exited the room. Mac quirked an eyebrow at his mom, but she simply shrugged and then walked over to gaze lovingly at her new granddaughter.

His brother Jason patted him on the back. "Nice side-step with the baby; for a minute there I thought you were going to cry."

Mac took the ribbing, but his mind was on his father. Was something wrong? "Is there a problem at the office I'm not aware of?" he asked his brother, ignoring his comment.

"Not that I know of," Jason said. "Why?"

"Probably nothing, but Dad got a call and sort of bolted from the room." Mac looked toward the doorway to see if his father had returned.

Before Jason could offer any input, Lily let out a small

cry and all attention was on the newborn. Mac never understood the attraction of babies, particularly newborns. They were tiny and wrinkly, fragile and terrifying, and they cried a lot. He watched in amazement as Lucas walked over and picked up his daughter with such gentleness that Mac almost couldn't look away. He was used to seeing Lucas being rough and physical; after all, years of high school sports and a career in the NFL had toughened him. But watching him now? He seemed at ease handling the tiny pink bundle and handing her to his wife. A collective sigh went out as Emma took the baby and cuddled her. Even Mac got a little misty at the sight of mother and child.

What in the world?

Taking a step back, he saw his father walking back into the room. "Everything okay, Dad?" William's face was drawn and sad. "Dad?"

William reached out and touched Mac's arm and pulled him aside. "Son," he said, his voice cracking slightly, "I need you to do something for me."

There were a million reasons why Gina Micelli should be anywhere else but where she was at the moment. She had a job that needed her, social engagements she had committed to, plants that needed to be watered, bills that needed to be paid...but the fact was that she was walking through the Charlotte Douglas International Airport on her way to see a man who had been vastly absent from her life for more than ten years.

Her father.

Arthur Micelli was a good father on paper; Gina had gone to the best schools and had a wardrobe that was the envy of all her friends. She vacationed all over the world and had a new car every three years. She had been given everything she had ever asked for.

Except his time.

Her parents had divorced when she was fifteen, her mother had taken her clear across the country, and her father had allowed it. Something she was still bitter about to this day.

She glanced down at the Rolex her father had given her for her last birthday and saw that it was just after two in the afternoon. She was scheduled to meet William Montgomery in baggage claim at two fifteen. That made her smile a little. The Montgomerys had always been such good friends to her parents, and Gina had nothing but fond memories of the countless times they had gotten together for barbecues and holidays and even several vacations.

She often thought about the family and where they all were now. She knew Lucas had played professional football, and although Gina was not a sports fan, she remembered reading about the injury that had ended his career. She had been devastated for her old friend and could only hope he was doing well. Jason Montgomery was a couple years older, and she had seen him several times in the last few years when he had flown out to the West Coast for business. It had never been intentional, but they ran in some of the same social circles, so she usually got the *Reader's Digest* version of what was new with his family.

While hearing how his parents were doing was always nice, she somehow managed to listen politely until he got to news about Mac.

Mackenzie Montgomery.

Sigh.

Mac had been her reason for living when she was a

teenager. He was so much older, and they had absolutely nothing in common, but she had always been drawn to him. He was serious and studious and much more reserved than his brothers, but Gina found that even at a young age, she was attracted to that in a man.

He had always been polite to her and had treated her like a kid sister, but by the time she hit puberty, the last thing she wanted was to have Mac think of her like that. Gina had had big plans for turning eighteen and how she would find the courage to engage with Mac on an adult level, but her mother had moved her thousands of miles away before she ever had the chance.

Sighing, Gina picked up her pace and navigated her way through the throngs of people to get to baggage claim. Her father was in serious condition and there was little hope of him living beyond the next three months. The thought caused a tightening in her chest. Even though Arthur Micelli was an absentee father, it didn't mean she wasn't devastated by the thought of losing him.

William had promised to set up an appointment for her to talk with her father's doctors, so they could better explain Arthur's condition. Gina was not particularly looking forward to that. She was here because Arthur was her father; she had no idea how to be with him or how she was supposed to act with his medical team. When she'd made arrangements at work for a leave of absence and her boss had asked how long she'd be gone, Gina had shrugged and said, "I don't know. A couple of weeks, I guess." Surely she wasn't expected to stay until the end? What good would that do? Wouldn't it be better for her and Arthur to settle their differences so that he could die in peace?

A shudder ran down her spine at her own callous thoughts. Gina couldn't think about her father dying, not now. She wasn't ready. In her mind, it was better to act as if he was going to recover and be okay.

Yes, that was what she was going to do. She would thank William for his efforts, but then graciously decline his offer to meet with the doctors. The less she knew, the better. No, her time would be better spent just being with her dad and making peace.

Looking up, she saw the signs for the carousel where her luggage would appear and anxiously looked around for William Montgomery. It had been well over ten years since she'd last seen him, but Gina had no doubt she'd recognize him. Her gaze went over the crowd of people standing around waiting, and that's when she saw him.

Mac.

What was Mac doing here? Where was his father? Why hadn't someone told her there had been a change in plans? She wasn't ready to meet up with the object of her every teenage fantasy. The flight had been over six hours; she stunk like plane and had dressed casually for the flight.

With a quick duck through the crowd, Gina ran for the nearest ladies room and did her best to freshen up. Her long, black hair had been haphazardly pulled back into a ponytail and the curls were begging to be let loose. Pulling the band from her hair, she shook it out and finger combed it to try and tame it. Unfortunately, the hair gods were not on her side and Gina thought she looked like something out of an eighties hair band video.

Sighing with frustration, she gave up the fight against her hair, pulled her small makeup bag from her purse, retouched her lipstick and blush, and used her travel toothbrush to do a quick brush and rinse to freshen her breath. The final touch was a spritz of perfume to her wrists, and then she straightened and turned to look at herself in the full-length mirror.

"Let's hope he doesn't hold too much stock in first impressions," she muttered as she squared her shoulders, took a deep breath, and made her way back out into the crowd and toward one Mackenzie Montgomery.

Mac scanned the crowd again in search of Gina Micelli. When his father had asked him if he would pick her up from the airport, Mac had been less than enthused at the idea, but it got him out of being part of the big taking-baby-Lily-home festivities.

It was like trading one form of hell for another.

It had been over ten years since he'd last seen Gina, and he basically had no idea who he should be looking for. He remembered her as a kid: dark hair, glasses, and the typical awkward, gangly teen. He may not know much about these things, but he was sure she wouldn't have stayed that way. Looking at his watch, he huffed with agitation. It was two twenty. He knew for a fact that Gina's plane had arrived on time, so where was she?

With another glance around the baggage claim area, he caught a glimpse of a gypsy. That was the only way to describe the woman who seemingly floated toward the luggage belt. She was petite—maybe five foot four, tops—and she wore some sort of long, gauzy black skirt that flowed with her every step. Peeking out from beneath the filmy fabric were a pair of bejeweled sandals and hot pink–tipped toes. Mac swallowed roughly as his gaze traveled upward.

She was wearing a sheer blouse, belted at the waist, and

underneath it was what promised to be a phenomenal body, covered in some sort of clingy teal-colored cami that matched the beaded necklace around her slender neck. Dark sunglasses covered her eyes, but Mac mentally bet himself they were either blue or green, and knew that either would look amazing against her tanned skin and jet-black hair.

He shifted his stance and pulled at the collar of his shirt because it certainly felt like it was getting hot in the airport. Unable to tear his eyes away, he watched, fascinated by her every graceful move, as she reached over and pulled a large black suitcase from the conveyor belt and then did her own scan of the crowd. When her gaze landed on him, Mac felt frozen to the spot.

Please don't let this be Gina, he cursed to himself.

Then she walked right up to him.

"Excuse me." Her soft voice washed over him like silk. "Mackenzie Montgomery?"

Mac looked down and almost groaned when his gypsy took off her sunglasses and eyed him warily. "Indeed I am," he said and hated how gruff his voice sounded. "It's good to see you again, Gina. I wish it were under better circumstances."

She looked down at the ground before meeting his gaze again. "Thank you," she replied softly. "Is your father here with you? He said he'd be the one meeting me."

Mac explained about Lucas and Emma and the baby, and he wasn't sure if he saw relief or annoyance on her face. Either way, her big green eyes were staring up at him, and he had to force himself to look away. "Here," he said after a long moment, "let me take your suitcase and we'll get going." When she didn't make a move right away, he stopped and looked at her. "Is it just the one bag?"

"What?" she asked, momentarily distracted by the enticing rear view of him. "Oh, yes, I tend to travel light."

"That's a first," he joked and started walking.

Gina had to take two steps for his every one and, when she caught up to him, asked, "What is that supposed to mean?"

He shrugged. "Nothing, it just always seems to me that women pack more than they'll ever need, no matter how long or short the trip. Based on that theory, I'd have to guess you don't plan on staying very long."

"I haven't really decided yet. I'm supposed to meet with some of my father's doctors tomorrow and discuss his prognosis, but honestly, I don't want to think about it. I'd rather focus on spending time with him now, rather than watching a clock that tells me when it's going to end."

Mac wasn't sure what to say to her. From what his father had told him, Arthur's prognosis was not good. He had stage four pancreatic cancer, and his heart was failing. Not a good combination. She looked to be holding up okay, but then again, he didn't really know Gina very well. Mac thought about how he'd feel if the tables were turned and it was his own father who was dying. He wasn't fool enough to believe William was going to be around forever, but the thought of knowing his time was so quickly coming to an end was enough to cause a deep ache around Mac's heart.

Pushing those thoughts aside, he decided to change the subject. "So, Dad tells me you'll be staying in the guesthouse."

Gina nodded. "I know I could stay at my father's house, but I've never been there and I just thought it would be odd. Plus no one else is there, and the thought of being alone in a strange house was a little bit intimidating."

Mac nodded in understanding.

"When your father offered me the use of your family's guesthouse, I was a bit surprised. I figured I'd just stay at a hotel and rent a car."

"My father would never have allowed that. He and Arthur have been friends since they were kids; you're like family. And family takes care of one another."

Just what she wanted to hear, another reference to her being like family. While she didn't mind it coming from William and Monica or even Lucas or Jason, the last thing she wanted was for Mac to think of her like a sister.

"Well, that's sweet of you to say," she said as they stepped out into the sunshine and she placed her sunglasses back on. "I'm very grateful for their hospitality. Plus, I have some very fond memories of the times our families spent together. It will be nice to stay someplace familiar."

Soon they were at Mac's car and Gina settled in as he put her suitcase in the trunk. When he climbed in beside her, it was as if the entire interior had shrunk. He was big—much bigger than the last time she'd seen him. Mac stood easily over six feet tall, and even in his monstrous SUV, he overpowered the space.

He didn't try to make small talk and for that Gina was thankful. As they made their way out of the airport parking lot, she took some time to observe him discreetly. Considering his intimidating frame, he moved with grace. His hands were large and tanned, and Gina secretly wished that he'd reach out with them to offer her some comfort.

But he didn't.

His dark brown hair was cut short and there wasn't a hair out of place. His suit was impeccable as well. She could tell Mac Montgomery was a man who liked order and organization. His car was spotless, his appearance was spotless, and she had a feeling he did not do well with any form of disorganization or chaos.

He'd think she was a hot mess.

She had no real plan for her time here; there was no schedule or itinerary. She had to simply go with the flow and take each day as it came until it was time for her to go. Gina knew it was just a gut feeling, but watching the rigid way Mac held himself reminded her of a person who did everything with a purpose and rarely relaxed.

With a sinking feeling in the pit of her stomach, she thought they'd probably make each other crazy if they spent too much time together.

Although making each other crazy could be fun.

A small smile tugged at her lips. While she had no idea how her days were going to go while she was in North Carolina, Gina knew she and Mac were bound to run into one another, especially if she was going to be staying at his parents' house.

"I don't know if my father mentioned it, but he and my mother are going to be out of town for part of your visit."

Gina nodded. "He did. He said he'd happily cancel their trip so I wouldn't be alone, but I told him that it wasn't the same thing as being alone at my father's. There I have no connection; it's a strange house I've never been to. With the guesthouse, it's part of my childhood. Plus, I didn't want them canceling their vacation on my account."

"Well, to be honest, he's really worried about Arthur."

She nodded again. "I know he is, but right now there isn't a whole lot any of us can do. Dad wouldn't want your father hovering over him at the hospital; that would make him crazy."

"It would make anyone crazy," Mac said a little too harshly. "I mean, your father has enough to deal with right now with medical staff hovering over him—he doesn't need any more spectators at this point."

"I hope that doesn't include me," she snapped.

"Of course not, Gina; you're his daughter."

"And your father is his best friend."

Mac sighed with frustration. Why were they even discussing this?

"There's a difference, and I think you know that. Your father is going to be happy to have you there with him after all this time." He realized immediately how that sounded. "What I mean is..."

Gina held up a hand to silence him. "It's okay, Mac. I know exactly how it is. My parents' marriage was a mess even before it ended, and by the time they decided to call it quits, it was unbearable even to be in the same room with them. I had no choice but to go with my mother to California; Dad didn't protest."

Mac was about to tell her they didn't have to talk about this, but he sensed that maybe Gina needed to.

"At first, my mother used the excuse that we needed time to settle in before letting me come back to North Carolina to visit with my father; then it was my school schedule. Dad came as often as he could, but his business kept him busy here on the East Coast. He made excuses and I pretended to understand, and in the long run, it meant that for the first time in a long time, no one was arguing. It was almost a relief..."

"I'm sorry," Mac said when Gina's voice trailed off. "That couldn't have been easy for you."

She shook her head. "It wasn't. Even when he did come

to visit, he never came to the house. I had to meet him other places, because if he and my mother got within ten feet of one another, they'd start fighting." The passing scenery held her attention for a few moments. "He was there for all of the important events, like my graduation from high school and college, but other than that, our time together was spotty. I think he believed that staying away was for the best."

"It was a difficult situation. There was probably never going to be a 'best' for anyone."

Gina turned and looked at Mac. "I think you're right," she said and then paused. "It still would have been nice if he had just asked."

This was all getting a little too deep for Mac. He liked and respected Arthur Micelli. He'd never given much thought to Arthur's estranged relationship with his daughter, and he didn't want to know this much personal information. Truth be known, Mac didn't like to get too deeply into anyone's personal life. It was easier that way. The less he knew, the better. Although he had plenty of friends and business associates, he never invited them to delve too deeply into his personal life, and he was rewarded with the same respect.

Before Gina launched into any more deep family secrets, Mac decided to change the subject. "My mother made sure the house was cleaned and stocked for you; you shouldn't need to do anything."

"That was nice of her," she said, seeming grateful for something lighter to talk about.

"Dad mentioned that you were getting a rental car. Is that really necessary? He has two spares I'm sure you could borrow, plus, with him and my mother going out of town, there'd technically be four cars for you to choose from."

Gina shook her head. "He mentioned that, but I really didn't want to impose any more than I already am. They're giving me a place to stay, and you came and got me from the airport...there comes a point where it feels like I'm taking advantage."

Why did women think this way? "You're not taking advantage, Gina. Trust me, no one will be using the cars and it's ridiculous for you to waste money on a car rental when you don't have to." His tone was firm and authoritative; he was certain that she'd agree with him.

"Well," she snapped, "ridiculous or not, that's how I feel. I didn't ask to be here or for a place to stay. I know how to take care of myself, and I don't need anyone telling me what to do!"

With a ragged sigh and mentally counting to ten, Mac softened his tone. "I'm not trying to tell you what to do. Really. I'm just trying to help you have one less thing to think about. This happened so quickly, I'm sure you're still trying to absorb it all."

He had her there. It had all happened quickly. One minute she was at work, worrying about getting financial statements filed for a difficult client, and the next she was packing a suitcase while making travel arrangements to get across the country to her father.

"Fine," she said begrudgingly. "I'll use one of their cars. I suppose it does make more sense."

Mac wanted to high-five himself but figured Gina wouldn't appreciate that. "Getting from my parents' place to the hospital is really easy. I don't imagine you'd remember your way around here that well."

She shrugged. "It's been so long, I'm sure things have changed."

"They have," Mac confirmed. "But like I said, the route

isn't difficult and all of his cars have navigation systems, so you shouldn't have any problems." She didn't respond and Mac was grateful for the silence. Within minutes, they were pulling into the circular driveway of his childhood home. "Here we are."

A wide smile crossed Gina's face and she turned to face Mac. "It looks exactly as I remembered it," she said in a voice laced with excitement. "It's weird. I don't remember much about the home I grew up in, but your house always stayed with me. Probably because to me, it was a refuge." She climbed from the car and almost took off at a run to get to the backyard—much like she had when she was a young girl.

Then she remembered that she wasn't a young girl anymore and there was a very serious-looking man watching her every move. Halting in her tracks, she turned and faced Mac. "It feels like only yesterday we were pulling up here for a barbecue. I used to love being here and running around back to the yard, where we would all swim and play volleyball. It was better than summer camp!"

Mac couldn't help but return her smile. "My folks loved having you around. I think my mom always felt a little gypped that she didn't have a daughter and ended up with three rambunctious boys; while you were here, she got to pretend."

Gina's heart softened at the thought. If only Monica knew how many times she had wished that she was a Montgomery too. "That's sweet. Although it seems like now she has quite a few girls in the picture to level the playing field." Mac looked at her quizzically, so she explained herself. "Well, with your brothers' wives, she has two daughters, and now she has a granddaughter too. All in all, I'll bet after those years of being tortured by her three sons, she's happy to finally have some women in the mix."

"You have no idea," Mac said with a laugh and grabbed Gina's luggage from the trunk. "C'mon, I'll show you to the guesthouse so you can get settled in."

"Thank you," she said and fell into step behind him.

Gina smiled as she walked along the stone path leading to the massive backyard and couldn't keep the grin off her face. The property had always been beautiful and all these years later, it still took her breath away. She paused to look at the small koi pond situated just inside the six-foot-tall gate. Yes, it was all still a feast for the eyes.

"Are you coming?" Mac asked, standing and watching her curiously.

Gina realized that she had been standing still for a few minutes. "Oh, sorry, yes," she replied and then watched as Mac walked away. He was all lean grace and solid muscle.

And another feast for her eyes.

Get Mac & Gina's story now:
https://www.chasing-romance.com/stay-with-me

And get the rest of the Montgomerys here:
https://www.chasing-romance.com/the-montgomery-brothers-series

ALSO BY SAMANTHA CHASE

The Donovans Series:

Dare Me

Tempt Me

The Magnolia Sound Series:

Sunkissed Days

Remind Me

A Girl Like You

In Case You Didn't Know

All the Befores

And Then One Day

Can't Help Falling in Love

Last Beautiful Girl

The Way the Story Goes

Since You've Been Gone

Nobody Does It Better

Wedding Wonderland

Always on my Mind

Kiss the Girl

Meet Me at the Altar:

The Engagement Embargo

With this Cake

You May Kiss the Groomsman

The Proposal Playbook

Groomed to Perfection

The I Do Over

The Enchanted Bridal Series:

The Wedding Season

Friday Night Brides

The Bridal Squad

Glam Squad & Groomsmen

Bride & Seek

The RoadTripping Series:

Drive Me Crazy

Wrong Turn

Test Drive

Head Over Wheels

The Montgomery Brothers Series:

Wait for Me

Trust in Me

Stay with Me

More of Me

Return to You

Meant for You

I'll Be There

Until There Was Us

Suddenly Mine

A Dash of Christmas

The Shaughnessy Brothers Series:

Made for Us

Love Walks In

Always My Girl

This is Our Song

Sky Full of Stars

Holiday Spice

Tangled Up in You

Band on the Run Series:

One More Kiss

One More Promise

One More Moment

The Christmas Cottage Series:

The Christmas Cottage

Ever After

Silver Bell Falls Series:

Christmas in Silver Bell Falls

Christmas On Pointe

A Very Married Christmas

A Christmas Rescue

Christmas Inn Love

The Christmas Plan

Life, Love & Babies Series:

The Baby Arrangement

Baby, Be Mine

Baby, I'm Yours

Preston's Mill Series:

Roommating

Speed Dating

Complicating

The Protectors Series:

Protecting His Best Friend's Sister

Protecting the Enemy

Protecting the Girl Next Door

Protecting the Movie Star

7 Brides for 7 Soldiers:

Ford

7 Brides for 7 Blackthornes:

Logan

Standalone Novels:

Jordan's Return

Catering to the CEO

In the Eye of the Storm

A Touch of Heaven

Moonlight in Winter Park

Waiting for Midnight

Mistletoe Between Friends

Snowflake Inn

His for the Holidays

Wildest Dreams (currently unavailable)

Going My Way (currently unavailable)

Going to Be Yours (currently unavailable)

ABOUT SAMANTHA CHASE

Samantha Chase is a New York Times and USA Today bestseller of contemporary romance that's hotter than sweet, sweeter than hot. She released her debut novel in 2011 and currently has more than eighty titles under her belt – including THE CHRISTMAS COTTAGE which was a Hallmark Christmas movie in 2017! She's a Disney enthusiast who still happily listens to 80's rock. When she's not working on a new story, she spends her time reading romances, playing way too many games of Solitaire on Facebook, wearing a tiara while playing with her sassy pug Maylene...oh, and spending time with her husband of 32 years and their two sons in Wake Forest, North Carolina.

Sign up for my mailing list and get exclusive content and chances to win members-only prizes!
https://www.chasing-romance.com/newsletter
Start a fun new small town romance series:
https://www.chasing-romance.com/the-donovans-series

Where to Find Me:
Website:
www.chasing-romance.com
Facebook:
www.facebook.com/SamanthaChaseFanClub

Instagram:
https://www.instagram.com/samanthachaseromance/
Twitter:
https://twitter.com/SamanthaChase3
Reader Group:
https://www.facebook.com/
groups/1034673493228089/

Made in United States
North Haven, CT
30 December 2023

46842026R00148